JUSTICE OF THE STAR

A JACK SAGE WESTERN - BOOK 7

DONALD L. ROBERTSON

Edited by
PAULINE NOLET

Illustrated by
DAMONZA.COM

COPYRIGHT

Justice of the Star

CM Publishing, LLC

Books@DonaldLRobertson.com

ISBN: 979-8-9912601-4-5

Formatted with Vellum

1

January 20, 1876

The northwest wind howled along the Dodge City main street, bouncing sleet from Jack's wide-brimmed Stetson. Pepper, the chestnut under him, held his head low, attempting to hide from the stinging crystals.

Jack, like his horse, was bent low, but his head moved from side to side, searching for the protection of a stable. The trip had been long and the weather tortuous. He had battled wind, rain, snow, and now sleet in his northern travel from Fort Smith, Arkansas. Reno Flint, the gunman he was after, was first rumored to have been in Abilene and then Ellsworth. Reaching Ellsworth, he was informed the man-in-black had moved west to Dodge City.

A stronger gust almost ripped his hat from his head. The knot, holding a bandanna wrapped over the top of his hat and ears and tied under his chin, finally gave up from the persistent hammering of the wind. The Stetson lifted, and only Jack's fast left hand smashing it to his head kept the wide-brimmed hat from sailing into the sleet-filled sky and disappearing into the white of the snow-covered prairie. Holding his hat with one hand

and Pepper's reins with the other, his eyes spotted a tall building with a loft and a large closed sliding door.

Even as he watched, the door slowly rolled open, and a large man waved, obviously in a hurry for him to get into the barn.

Jack laid the reins over, guiding Pepper toward the open door, but it wasn't necessary. The horse had turned for the opening. The other two horses and the mule on leads had been slogging along behind them. Now, spotting the welcoming warmth, Stonewall picked up his pace, passing Pepper and stepping into the lead.

"I know, boys. I'm as ready as you to get out of this mess." Jack bumped Pepper to hurry him along, but he needed little urging. With the others alongside, Pepper trotted through the gaping opening and halted in the protection of the stable.

Once the animals were inside, the big door rumbled, banging in the wind, as the man shoved it closed. He dropped a locking bolt and walked toward Jack, who was swinging out of the saddle. In almost a growl, the man said, "Not a good day to be out for a ride, feller."

Jack, his left hand still gripping the crown of his hat and bandanna, lifted his Stetson from his head. After sticking the bandanna into a pocket, he shoved a hand inside the hat and reshaped the tall crown where the pressure from his big hand had smashed it almost flat. He tapped the top with the edge of his hand to reestablish the creases. Using both hands, one on the front of the brim and one on the back, he leveled the hat on his head. After positioning it, he turned to the liveryman. "Mister, you are the master of understatement. This is some of the most miserable weather I've been in. I'm ready for some sunshine, and so are my animals."

The liveryman stood at least two inches taller than Jack, with a chest like a barrel. In his wool overcoat, his arms jutted out from his body like two fence posts. Hair hung to his shoulders, and the lower half of his face was covered with a thick black beard. A giant, he outweighed Jack by at least fifty pounds. "Ain't as bad as I've seen it. Reckon it'll get plenty worse afore it gets better."

He looked at the four animals and spoke in the same gruff voice. "You got some big stock. They'll eat more'n normal. It'll be twenty cents a day for boarding. That includes hay and water. Add ten cents if you want corn or oats."

The man's tone was brusque, rubbing Jack the wrong way, but he ignored it. His animals were cold, they needed attention, and so did he. "How much for a week?" Jack expected a discounted flat fee for a week, but the liveryman held his gaze.

The big man spit and wiped his mouth with the back of his gloved hand before he spoke. "Listen, cowboy, if you multiply that twenty or thirty cents a day times seven days and four animals, you'll have it. I don't give discounts for my work. One day, seven days, a month, I still have to work. It ain't discounted. For all four of those animals"—he gave Stonewall a particularly hard look—"if you want the mule to get the same treatment, for a week it'll be five dollars and sixty cents, or eight dollars and forty cents if you're hankerin' after corn or oats."

Jack thought, *This guy is the least friendly cuss I've met in a long time*. He looked around and noticed, even on a day like today, there were quite a few empty stalls. This place didn't appear to be too popular. That probably meant there was another livery in town. He paid Blackbeard for a couple of days and, during that time, would find the other stable. "Two days. Hay, corn, and oats. I'd like blankets over all of them, including the mule. They've gotten mighty cold out there."

The man scratched the right side of his black beard. "If'n you want corn *and* oats, it'll be an additional nickel. Also, the blankets are ten cents apiece per day. That'll make it a buck-fifty a day." The man stopped scratching and held Jack's gaze with challenging blue eyes.

Jack shook his head, an edge to his reply. "Then make it two days. The way I figure it, that's three dollars." He unbuttoned his overcoat, then his coat. When he could reach into his vest pocket, he pulled out three paper bills and shoved them into the liveryman's outstretched hand. "Does the price include rubdowns, or is that also extra?"

"Nope, it ain't extra." He untied the leads of the two horses and mule from Jack's saddle.

"Hold it." Jack's voice was sharp. He took Smokey's and Stonewall's leads from the man and gave him Pepper's reins. "I'll take the mule and the grulla. Smokey and Stonewall have been with me a long time."

The man's head shot up at the mention of Stonewall's name. He glared at Jack, his beard-covered chin jutting out. "You a reb? I don't cotton to rebs. I fought for the north."

Jack had been applying diligent effort to keep calm at the man's rude manner, but with the last question, he had had enough. His voice was hard when he asked, "Is there another stable in town?"

"You ain't going nowhere until you answer me, boy. In fact, you bein' a reb, why don't I just beat your answer out of you?"

Jack shook his head in disgust. He doubted this loudmouth had even served. When Jack left the service, he had carried the rank of major in the northern cavalry, but he owed no explanation to the bully. All he wanted was to find out if there was another stable in town. "I asked you a question, mister. Give me an answer."

Above the beard, the man's face turned beet red. He dropped the horses' leads, and his fists clenched into massive clubs. Taking two steps toward Jack, he said, "You're gonna regret yore last words, boy. Nobody demands anything from Bruiser Bailey. You've been getting by on your size, but not today. I'm gonna show you just what can happen to a smart-mouthed reb like you."

It had been a long ride, and Jack, like his animals, was tired and cold, especially his feet. Several times, he had gotten out of the saddle and walked to keep them from freezing. This loudmouth had drained his last bit of patience. He could feel his anger, cold as the weather outside, beginning to flood his body, but his hands were cold and stiff from the exposure. The last thing he wanted to do was hit anyone with his fists. Disgusted with the bully, Jack decided to put as quick an end to this as possible, cold extremities or not.

The liveryman's right arm cocked, and his left foot moved forward for more leverage in his blow. His last words were barely out of his mouth when the toe of Jack's left boot, driven with all the force a long muscled leg could muster, struck the big man's crotch with unerring accuracy. The man's previous step had opened him up perfectly. Jack's opponent lifted completely off the ground.

The sound of the sickening thud, like a sledgehammer bursting a watermelon, filled the stable. A whoosh of air escaped the big man. He doubled over and, with both hands clutching his groin, toppled to the ground. He lay in the sawdust moaning while Jack pried the hand clinching the bills open and retrieved his three dollars.

"I asked you if there's another livery in town."

Through the moans, the man gasped, "Up the street on the right, Clements and Sons." He muttered again, his voice a plea, "I need a doctor."

Jack calmly took out his bandanna, wrapped it tight over the crown of his hat, and tied it under his chin. He buttoned both coats, pulled the collars close around his neck, and strode to the big door. After pulling the locking bolt, he shoved the door wide enough so his string of animals could pass. Making his way back to his animals, he gathered the leads, picked up Pepper's reins, and swung into the saddle.

The liveryman moaned again. "You ain't gonna leave me here, are you?" His tone was much less demanding than earlier.

Ignoring him, Jack turned Pepper to the opening. Reluctantly, the big chestnut started for the door. The leads tightened, and his other animals made their way behind him into the storm. Passing through the wide-open door, Jack thought, *I oughta let you freeze to death, but I won't do that to the other animals.* He swung to the ground, shoved the door closed, climbed back into the saddle, and again turned Pepper into the freezing wind.

The dull light making its way through the clouds and sleet illuminated a deserted street. No one ventured out. He rode until nearly reaching the opposite end of town before seeing the Clements and Sons livery through the heavy sleet, which was again combined with snow.

The livery wasn't as big as the one where Jack had first stopped, but he figured whoever was inside couldn't help but be more welcoming. He sidled Pepper to the door and banged on it. Within seconds, the door rolled open. Soon, there was sufficient space for Jack and his animals to slip inside. Once they were clear, the door reversed direction and was closed by the time Jack stepped from the saddle.

A young, blond-headed boy of about seventeen, wearing a heavy overcoat and gloves, jogged up to Jack. "Morning, mister. Mighty cold out there. Come to think of it, it ain't that warm in here. Name's Rodney Clements. Folks call me Roddy. Looks like you got some nice animals here." He ran his hand over Stonewall's shoulder. "Mighty fine mule. My pa raises mules. Fine animals. You staying tonight or longer?"

"Shouldn't you be in school, boy?"

"No, sir. The teacher let school out 'cause of the weather. Folks gotta care for their livestock, but I'm about out, anyway. This is my last year. When I'm done, I'm gonna trail down to Texas and join me up to a cattle drive. Reckon that'll be fun."

Jack shook his head. *Thursday,* he thought. *I've been doing so much traveling, I've lost track of days.* "Roddy, is today the twentieth?"

"Yes, sir. January twentieth, eighteen hundred and seventy-six.

Ain't that something? We've been a country for nigh on a hundred years."

Jack nodded. "That's something, Roddy." He patted Pepper on the shoulder. "Roddy, you have room for these boys?"

"We surely do."

"Good. Let's get them unloaded, rubbed down, and blankets for all of them. They've been cold for quite a while."

Roddy nodded and led Stonewall to the first open stall and then returned for Smokey, placing him next to the mule. Jack led Pepper and Thunder into their stalls and began stripping the gear from the red horse. "Got a place for this gear?" he called to Roddy.

"Tack room's behind the office. If you want, you can just pile it by the office, and I'll be glad to put it up for you. Feel free to leave anything and everything. It'll be safe here. Never had anyone steal from Pa. He's a fair man, but he don't abide thieves. Robbers leave him be."

Jack began rubbing down Pepper. "Good to know. I'll probably be here for a while. What do you folks charge?"

"Pa don't believe in charging too much." He stopped rubbing Stonewall, raised his head, and looked at Jack. "Unlike some folks I know. It'll be two bits a day. That includes everything, even corn and oats. Stay a week and it's a buck fifty."

Jack was about to ask more questions when the smaller door at the front, next to the big rolling door, opened, and two men stepped inside. The first man had the look of a lawman. On his heels followed the liveryman Jack had put down, walking with an awkward, swinging shuffle.

The boy stopped what he was doing and jerked to his full height. "Bailey, you ain't welcome here. Get yourself out." Roddy frowned at the man in the lead. "Marshal, you know Pa don't allow Bailey or his bunch in this livery, and he left me in charge. He expects me to enforce his rules. So get him outta here."

Before the marshal could respond, Bailey spoke up, his voice loud and gravelly. "Shut up, boy, or I'll come over there, pull yore pants down, and give you the whipping yore smart mouth deserves."

At his comments, the marshal spun around and pointed a gloved finger at him. "Bruiser, you shut your mouth, or you'll be outside. Now, is this the man?" He nodded toward Jack.

Bruiser Bailey's attention jerked to Jack, and his thick arm shot out, his finger aimed at Jack. "That's him, Marshal. He kicked me in the privates for no reason a-tall. I was just tryin' to help him get his animals out of this bad weather. I may be ruined for life."

Throughout Bailey's venting, the marshal kept his eyes on Jack. When he finished, the lawman said, "What do you have to say about that, mister . . .?"

Jack had gone back to Pepper's rubdown while Bailey was talking. With the marshal's question, he stopped, straightened, and laid his arms across Pepper's back, so both hands were in sight. "Jack Sage, Marshal. What's your name?"

"Taylor, Mr. Sage. Craig Taylor. As you can hear, Mr. Bailey says you assaulted him in an unprovoked attack. You care to explain?"

Roddy interrupted. "Marshal, I asked you politely to get rid of Bailey. You know if my pa was here, he'd already thrown him out."

Marshal Taylor, his patience running thin, stared at Roddy for a second, then turned to Bailey. "He's right, Bruiser. You go on out of here. You can wait outside or in my office."

"But Marshal, it's cold out there."

"It's not cold in my office. You know what would happen if you were dealing with Gideon Clements. You'd be leaving at the point of a shotgun. So go on, like Roddy says."

Bailey glared at Roddy. "Yore mouth's gonna get you in big trouble, kid." He waited for a reply from the boy, but Roddy said nothing, only returning Bailey's glare. When no response was forthcoming, he slowly turned and pushed through the door into the waiting wind.

Once the door slammed shut, Marshal Taylor turned to Jack, who had returned to drying Pepper's rear leg. "Mr. Sage, you mind answering my question?"

Jack straightened and again laid his arms across Pepper's back. "He's right about one thing, Marshal Taylor. I kicked him just about as hard as I could, and I'll tell you, it was mighty gratifying. I have to admit he's tougher than I expected. A lesser man would have been on the floor of that barn for the rest of the day." The marshal's mustache covered most of his upper lip and the corners of his mouth, but Jack could swear he saw Taylor's mustache twitch with his comments.

"You just hauled off and kicked him?"

"No, sir, I did no such thing. That man is almighty rude. I stopped at his place because it was on the side of town I rode in from. As soon as I got inside, I realized it was a mistake. That fella doesn't seem to care much for other people. It looked like he thought little of mules either, but when I mentioned my mule's name, Stonewall, he got downright insulting. In fact, he made fists and stepped toward me in a threatening manner. I allow no man to lay hands on me, so I just naturally applied the toe of my boot where it would do the most good, and that's the complete story. He was coming at me, and I stopped him."

Marshal Taylor nodded. "That's good enough for me. Bailey has a bad rep. Several of his customers have got crossways with him, and he's beaten them badly. One almost died, but the folks who get beat up never file a complaint, and it seems they're always in the wrong. Maybe this'll slow him down a little."

Jack shook his head. "I doubt it. I've run into men like him. They use their size to intimidate others. They enjoy it. Bailey's type never changes."

"You could be right. Be careful. He might want a rematch, and like you said, he's a tough hombre." The marshal tipped his hat and turned to go.

"Marshal?" Jack said.

The man stopped. "Yeah?"

Jack had unbuttoned his coats. He pulled them back, exposing the badge on his vest. "I'm a U.S. Marshal."

"I thought I had heard the name before. You were out in Wyoming."

Jack nodded. "I'm looking for a man, a gunfighter. Name's Reno Flint. He's big and dresses in black. It's possible Flint could have already left your town, but with this weather, I suspect he might still be here. He killed a man in Missouri, and I have a warrant for his arrest. It's said he is quick with a gun and supposedly has a temper to match his speed."

2

With the mention of Flint's name, Roddy, working on Stonewall, jerked to a stop and looked first at the marshal and then Jack. His head slanted toward a big black gelding standing in a far stall with a blanket draped over him. "That's Mr. Flint's horse. He seems like a good man, other than wearing all that black."

Marshal Taylor smoothed his mustache with the thumb and forefinger of his left hand. "I'll have to agree with the boy. We've got a bunch of troublemakers in town, but Reno hasn't been one of them. He deals a game of poker in the Long Branch. There's been no complaints about him. His size keeps most of the trouble from even starting. I'm sure that's something you're familiar with." Taylor paused while Jack gave him a brief nod.

Yep, Jack thought, *my size has kept me out of quite a few fights and helped me settle others pretty quickly.*

Taylor continued, "You two look to be near the same size. He might be a smidgen bigger than you. Like you, I've heard he's fast, but haven't seen him in action. He's been pretty peaceable since he arrived. In fact, he's stopped a couple of disagreements that could've turned violent." The sheriff shrugged. "Course, he's only been here a few days."

Roddy spoke up. "A week. He rode in exactly a week ago, late in the evening. I was working. He asked for a good place to stay, and I sent him to the Harbor Hotel."

Jack finished with Pepper and started moving to Thunder, but slid to a stop and stared at Roddy. "Did you say Harbor Hotel? The closest harbor is about a thousand miles from here."

The boy shrugged. "My uncle was on the sea for a few years, and that's what he named his hotel. I guess it makes sense to him."

Jack moved on to Thunder and began drying the gray gelding. "So I suppose you're recommending it?"

The boy nodded. He looked across the grulla's back. "Yes, sir. Sheets are clean, and the price is reasonable. They've also got a good eating place." He rushed on. "I ain't recommending it 'cause it's family. It's just a good place to stay."

Jack shook his head. "Never thought different, Roddy. It was the name that caught me." He glanced at the town marshal. "I'll be hanging around town until I figure out what I'm going to do about Flint. I have a warrant, so I'll at least need to talk to him, and I may be using your jail. I'd appreciate it if you'd keep the warrant to yourself." He looked at the boy. "You too, Roddy."

Taylor nodded. "No problem. Just try not to get shot. It gets pretty lively around here in the evenings. I'll see you around, and you best keep an eye open for Bailey. He latches onto a grudge and won't let go." He pulled his coat tight and turned for the door. "See you, Roddy."

The boy nodded. "So long, Marshal."

Wind whipped around the door, pushing big snowflakes to the rafters. Taylor slammed it closed, and the flakes circled around for a few moments until they gradually floated to the straw below.

With Marshal Taylor gone, Roddy and Jack worked until they

finished the horses. Jack moved his gear to the tack room and picked up his saddlebags, bedroll, and rifle. He stepped out of the tack room and watched Roddy feeding his horses and mule. *The boy's a hard worker,* he thought, *and he likes the animals. I'm glad I didn't leave them back at Bailey's.*

He stooped, laid the bedroll on the wooden deck built around the office and tack room, and gently propped his rifle across the bedroll. Then he opened his saddlebags, searched inside, and drew out five horse cookies. After closing it, he swung the heavy bags over his shoulder. He moved to Pepper, and before he could reach the horse's head, it turned to look at him. "Did you smell this, boy?" He extended one of the cookies, and the red horse took it gently. The horse's big tongue moved the cookie around until it was positioned just right, and he started crunching. Jack patted him twice on the shoulder and moved to Thunder.

After giving a cookie to each, he tossed the last one to Roddy.

The boy caught the cookie and turned it over, examining it. "What's this?"

Jack returned to the deck, buttoned his coats, and pulled his collars up before picking up his rifle and bedroll. "Roddy, that's the best horse cookie meant for man. I'm not kidding. Those things are tasty. Try it out. You'll like it."

After examining the cookie, Roddy broke off an edge and popped it into his mouth. Jack watched the grin grow across his face.

"Not bad, huh?"

"That's mighty good, Marshal Sage." He put another piece in his mouth and chewed, moving it around so he could talk. "Mighty good." He looked at the animals. "Looks like they like 'em, too. Is it a secret recipe?"

Jack shook his head. "Nope, I'll share it with you after I eat and look around. Now tell me how to get to this Harbor Hotel."

Roddy trotted to the door to open it for Jack. "Head back the way you came. It's the fifth building on this side of the street, just before you get to the Long Branch." Before he pulled the latch and opened the door, he gave Jack an intense look. "I'd surely like to have seen you kick Bruiser Bailey. He's deserving of every ounce of pain you gave him."

Interesting, Jack thought. *There are some hard feelings in Dodge City between Bailey and the Clements.*

Roddy pulled the big door open only wide enough for Jack to step through. The wind was stronger, and the sleet was gone, but the snow was thicker and blowing sideways. "Have a good day, Marshal," Roddy called, his voice fragmented by the wind as Jack held his hat to his head and turned down the boardwalk, holding close to the buildings.

Though the morning had progressed, he made it to the Harbor Hotel without seeing another person. He pushed through the double doors, made sure they were tightly latched, and headed for the front desk. Reaching it, he untied his bandanna, tied it around his neck, and removed his crumpled hat. While straightening the crown of the Stetson, he surveyed the lobby, his gaze ending on the elderly man watching him from across the counter. "Good morning."

The old man followed his efforts on his hat through red, watery eyes. Suddenly, he yanked a well-used handkerchief from his coat pocket, held it up to his bulbous red nose, which presided over a neatly trimmed beard and mustache, and blasted a sneeze into it. When he was finished wiping the almost raw appendage, he coughed, cleared his throat, returned the handkerchief to his pocket, and rasped, "I reckon."

Jack gave the old man a long look. "You oughta be curled up in bed, sipping a hot toddy, old-timer."

The man started to respond, but instead yanked the handkerchief from his pocket again. It reached his nose only moments before he blasted another sneeze. He continued with two more before wiping his nose. He returned the handkerchief to his pocket and shoved the hotel register across to Jack, along with the pen and ink.

"You ain't half-wrong, mister. I wouldn't be working today, but my nephew's sick. He normally works the desk this time of day."

Jack picked up the damp pen, dipped it, and signed his name. Once he finished, he returned the pen to its holder and removed his gloves, shoving them into a coat pocket.

The old man spun the ledger, looked at Jack's name, coughed once, and moved his gaze from the ledger to Jack. "Welcome, Marshal Sage. How long you expecting to be here?"

"At least a week. How much?"

The old man cleared his throat. "Three bucks a day, but if you're staying for seven days, you'll get the last day for free, a total of twelve dollars."

Jack gladly unbuttoned his two coats to access his money, for the heat in the lobby had his overcoat steaming. Glancing at the roaring fireplace, he removed the heavy overcoat, reached past the lighter coat into his vest pocket, and retrieved a gold eagle and two silver dollars. Dropping the coins on the ledger, he motioned his head to the restaurant. "How's the food?"

The question brought a smile to the man's face. "The best you'll find in Kansas. My niece learned her skills from her ma and a big restaurant in New York City. She ran it for 'em for several years. We was lucky to get her to leave the city and return here."

Jack looked at the bleary red eyes and could see the pride in them. "You a Clements?"

"I am. Why do you ask?"

"I left my horses with your nephew. Seems to be a fine young fella, and he was taking good care of them."

"Roddy's first-rate. He's the responsible type, and there ain't many of those around in these here progressive times. Gideon, that's his pa, my brother, he taught him well."

"You the one who named this hotel?"

The old man's face hardened behind the wrinkles, mustache, and beard, his eyes growing suspicious, head tilted a bit. "I am."

Jack grinned. "Pretty accurate name for out here in this sea of grass. Speaking of sea, I understand you spent time on it."

Clements's face softened. "Reckon I did. Shipped out of Norfolk long before the war. Rejoined the family when it started. I'm sure you understand the need for that, Marshal."

"I do, Mr. Clements."

The old man reached behind him, pulled a key from the cubbies, and dropped it on the register. "Call me Cap. You're upstairs toward the back on the east side."

"Cap, isn't the Long Branch on that side?"

Clements sneezed again, his head nodding. "Yep, but that fierce wind is comin' out of the northwest. This place is built as tight as possible, but the wind we're having now, it'll make it through most any plank wall. You being on the east side, you'll be warmer."

Jack picked up the key and dropped it into his vest pocket. "Then the east side it is. Much obliged." He picked up his bedroll and saddlebags, set them on the counter, and laid his overcoat over the top. "Cap, you mind if I leave these things with you while I grab a bite to eat?"

The hotel owner gave a nod. "Glad to take 'em, and I'll take care of that rifle if you've a mind to."

Jack handed the Winchester across the counter. "Careful, there's one in the oven."

The old man chuckled. "Wouldn't be much good to you if there weren't."

Jack watched Cap place his gear in the corner next to the cubby cabinet. "Much obliged," he said, and turned toward the restaurant. Stepping through the arched doorway from the hotel to the restaurant, he was surprised at the amount of business they had on a day like today. Patrons occupied every table. He was about to return to the lobby and grab a seat in one of their lounge chairs, but a man sitting alone at a table near the front waved to him.

The man spoke as Jack neared the table. "Join me. There's plenty of room."

"Thanks. I'm surprised it's so crowded in here. I figured most folks would be huddled around their fireplaces today."

The stranger shook his head. "Gotta make a living, no matter what kind of weather we got. Most of these folks have businesses. With the sleet and snow this morning, they're just a little slow getting to them."

Jack pulled out a chair and extended his hand to the man. "I'm Jack Sage, obliged for your hospitality."

The man took his hand in a firm grip. "Norm Caster. I'm in town to pick up some supplies. I've got a place west of here."

Jack pulled his beat-up Stetson from his head, looked at it for a moment, and placed it on the vacant side of the table. "You picked a fine day to come into town, Mr. Caster."

The corners of the man's eyes crinkled, and the left side of his mouth rose, lifting the curl in his handlebar mustache. "Never claimed to be the smartest man in the world." One eyebrow also lifted as his dark brown eyes settled on Jack. "By the by, Mr. Sage, looks like you're doing a little traveling today yourself."

Jack raised his hands, grinning at his accuser. "Guilty as charged. I guess neither of us can lay claim to the smartest-man title."

Caster chuckled. "Quite a pair we are. Call me Norm."

The click of heels and the sound of a swishing skirt sounded behind Jack, while the sweet smell of flowered perfume and cooked bread enveloped the table. His mind jerked him back to the woman he loved, who waited for him in Fort Smith, Grace Blakely. She smelled much the same as this lady. He remembered the kiss Grace gave him for a going-away present, the warmth of her full lips. Jack blinked to clear his mind and watched Norm.

His face brightened, and he broke into a wide smile. "Morning, Bess. You're looking mighty pretty today."

She stepped around where she could see both men. Her cheeks brightened at Norm's compliment, and her hazel eyes tightened. Her reply was stiff. "Thank you, Norm. The usual?"

"Yes, ma'am. I'm a creature of habit."

She turned to Jack. "Good morning, sir. I'm Elizabeth Taylor, but everyone calls me Bess. What can I get you?"

Jack's stomach gave a loud growl.

Though Bess tried to keep the giggle in, it burst forth. She followed up quickly. "It sounds like you would like everything on the menu."

Jack grinned at her quip and at Norm's laughter. "I am hungry, Bess, but *everything* might be a bit much." He glanced out the windows at the blowing snow. "As cold as it is, I don't imagine you have any eggs."

She flashed a warm smile. "Fortunately, sir, you are wrong. We do have eggs, and we also have fresh bacon, and today, I can promise you cold milk."

"Cold milk sounds mighty good, but how about adding some hot coffee, and I'm sure you've got some cream back there. Four eggs, a stack of bacon so crisp if you dropped it on the floor it'd shatter like your mother's China, and whatever else you have to go with it. I'm a hungry man this morning."

"The cook just mixed up some flapjacks if you would care for a stack."

"That and some hot biscuits would sure chase away the cold."

She gave him a friendly smile, inclined her head toward Norm, and made her way through the crowded tables toward the kitchen.

Jack observed Norm keeping a protective eye on her, weaving her way around the crowded tables until she had disappeared through the swinging door.

Moments later, she returned with a steaming pot of hot coffee and a small pitcher of cream. After placing the pitcher on the table near Jack, she poured coffee into his cup.

"Thanks, Bess, that'll do," Jack said, stopping her when the cup was only about two-thirds filled.

She moved to Norm's cup, filled it, and placed the pot of coffee on a brass trivet between the two men. She nodded toward the pot. "That'll get cold if you don't drink up. When it does, wave, and I'll get you a fresh pot. Your breakfasts will be out shortly."

Jack slid the sugar bowl closer and began using the sugar spoon like a shovel. He could see Norm's eyes tracking Bess, but as he dumped the third spoonful into his cup, his new acquaintance changed his focus to Jack's cup and leaned closer. "You having a little coffee with your sugar this morning?"

Jack shoveled another spoonful into his cup, dropped the sugar spoon back in the bowl, and reached for the cream, filling the remaining space. Next, he picked up his spoon and stirred the mixture, careful not to slosh any over the edge. With a steady hand, he lifted the cup to his lips, took a long sip, and set it down, turning to his companion. "That's a mighty original question, Norm."

Norm grinned. "I guess you've heard it before, what with all the sugar you use."

Jack took another sip of coffee and shook his head in mock disgust. "You have no idea."

Both men laughed before he took another sip. Jack was facing the windows and could see the snow beginning to thin. The wind was still howling, but the buildings across the street stood out in stark clarity, no longer mere shadows visible only between flurries.

Heels clicking again, Bess approached with a large tray holding both men's breakfasts. Norm jumped to his feet to give her a hand.

With forehead wrinkled and brown eyes snapping, she thrust

her body between Norm and the tray and tossed a quick glance around the room. "Sit down, Norm. I can handle this myself."

He sheepishly lowered himself back into his chair.

She smiled at Jack. "Sorry, sometimes Norm gets a little too protective."

Jack kept his mouth shut, and his eyes tracked the big plate of eggs, bacon, and biscuits, with a white gravy on the side, plus a tall stack of pancakes. Reaching for his knife and fork, he smiled at Bess. "It looks mighty good, ma'am."

"Thank you." She glanced at Norm, the smile continuing while she turned to head to another table. "If you two need anything, just wave."

Norm watched her go before grinning at Jack. "Spirited, ain't she?"

Jack, his mouth full, declined to answer, only nodding.

After quickly working his way through the eggs, bacon, biscuits, gravy, and pancakes, he was feeling better. He leaned back in his chair and watched Norm for a moment. The man was bigger than average. He wore his gun like he could use it, and looked to be in his late twenties or early thirties. He had an open, honest face, and the build of a hardworking man, but he had that look about him. Jack felt sure he had been a lawman some time in his past.

Norm sliced a chunk from his steak and shoved it into his mouth. After chewing for a moment, he swallowed and caught Jack looking at him. "What's up?"

Jack took a sip of his coffee. "I was wondering. You mentioned you have a place west of here. I figured most folks with ranches would be out trying to save their stock in this weather."

"And I'm not."

Jack nodded.

"That's because I'm no rancher. The only stock I have, a milk cow and a couple of mules, are closed up in the barn where they won't drift in this weather, with plenty of feed and water. Course, I'll have to be getting back to make sure the watering trough don't freeze up. I'm a farmer."

3

Jack sat back in his chair, his eyes on the man who had just labeled himself a farmer. He picked up his coffee cup, drew it to his lips, and took a long sip. Holding his cup in both hands, he surveyed Norm through the steam rising above the coffee. "Now that surprises me. You don't look like a farmer."

Norm grinned. "How does a farmer look?"

Jack shook his head, placing the cup on the table. "It's not so much how a farmer looks, but how you look. You'd pass for a lawman with no questions asked."

Norm glanced outside. "Snow's stopped."

It had, but the wind continued to howl, rattling shutters and blowing loose snow into the air, still not a pleasant day.

The farmer continued, "After the war, I spent several years as town marshal and got elected to sheriff for a while. Only did one term, and I walked away. Had to kill one boy and hang another. Lawing wasn't my kind of work. I had enough killing in the war. My pa was a farmer, and I've always liked it, so I moved out here and bought a parcel of land." One side of Norm's mustache rose again in a sideways grin, and he shrugged. "That's pretty much it. How long you been packing a badge?"

Jack opened his mouth to answer, but an icy blast of wind flooded the dining room, followed by the sound of loud laughter, a ribald comment, and the slamming of the hotel door.

Norm sighed. "Sounds like it might be trouble. The restaurant gets a lot of business from the Long Branch."

Jack moved his chair, adjusting his coat so he could reach the Smith & Wesson riding in his right holster. His hand moved to the weapon and checked it was riding easy and free. With his left, he picked up his coffee cup. It was rock steady. He took one last sip and set it down.

Four cowhands staggered into the dining room. They surveyed the full tables, and one of them threw back his head and bellowed, "Bess!"

Jack watched her walk through the opening from the kitchen. Her demeanor was as calm as if she were walking into church.

Reaching the group, her back stiffened, and her forehead wrinkled in a frown. "Lester, you are drunk."

The young cowhand who had so loudly called her name flashed a wide, toothy grin. "I sure am, Bess, and I'm mighty hungry, too."

The other three nodded in agreement. Lester was evidently the spokesman for this noisy little gang.

"Why don't you run some of these city folks out of here so hardworking cowhands can get a little grub?"

With his first glance, Jack had registered these four men as exactly what they claimed to be: drunk, hungry, hardworking cowhands. They'd be no problem if they were handled correctly, and it looked like Bess was doing a fine job. He had turned so he could see outside, watch the cowhands with just a corner of his eye, and keep a watch on Norm. Having already shown his protectiveness toward Bess, if the cowhands got rowdy, Jack figured Norm would jump in. The man was already sitting on the edge of his chair. Then Lester glanced their way.

"Well, shoot, Bess. There's only two of those sodbusters at that big ole table, and look at all those empty dishes. Why, they've finished. They can move along and make room for us."

This could be the fuse, Jack thought. He leaned slightly toward Norm. "Easy, Norm. There's no need to have anything start." Jack could see the concern on Bess's face. *She's worried, too,* he thought.

Lester turned and, with the other three staggering in behind him, zigzagged his way toward them on unsteady legs. "Hey, sodbusters, why don't you let some fine, upstanding cowpunchers have your table?"

Jack saw Norm stiffen. He spoke low to his companion. "Forget it, Norm. They're just kids. We're through, anyway. Let me handle it. Just follow my lead."

Norm took a deep breath and nodded. Jack could see his companion was ready for a fight, guns or fists, and he wanted no dustup in this crowded dining room.

Lester reached the table first, and as he was opening his mouth, Jack stood to his full height and spun around to face the young men. All four slid to a stop, and their heads snapped back as they stared up at Jack.

He gave Lester a wide grin. "I bet you boys are hungry after a long night of drinking."

Lester stared up at the giant who had just sprung up before him, wearing a wide, engaging grin.

Jack silently chuckled at the boy's consternation. "Well, speak up, fella. Aren't you hungry?"

Lester partially regained his composure. He blurted out, "We sure are, and it's time for you—"

Jack, his grin never leaving his face, grabbed Lester by his coat and slammed him into the chair he had just vacated. "Well, sit. We were just leaving." He looked toward Bess, motioning her over. Next, his eyes fell on the other three, stopping at each one.

Though his grin remained, his eyes were cold and hard, and his voice carried a commanding tone. "Sit down, boys. Fill those empty bellies."

Having lost their bravado, the other three cowhands scattered around the table and sat. One of them picked up Jack's hat. "This your hat, mister?"

Jack took the beat-up Stetson. "Thanks. You boys have a fine breakfast. Maybe I can buy you a drink sometime." He turned to Bess. "How much do we owe you, Miss Bess?"

The cowhands sat silently at the table.

"Two dollars for you, and one for Norm."

Jack pulled out a half eagle and dropped it into Bess's hand. "Thank you, ma'am. Keep the change." He turned to Norm. "Let's go."

Norm grinned at Bess. "See you around."

She gave a quick, furtive look around the room before a brief smile was tossed to him. "You be careful. It's cold out there."

The two men left the dining room. There was no whooping or yelling from the drunken cowhands. They had quieted, and just the low rumble of conversation could be heard from the other patrons.

Reaching the hotel lobby, Norm stopped at a clothes tree, carefully removed his hat and coat from the overloaded stand, and slipped them on. "That was pretty slick. There for a minute, I thought we might tangle with those boys, but you sure took the steam out of them."

Jack shook his head. "I didn't figure them for desperadoes. They got liquored up and were feeling their oats. Lester was the key. Once he was quieted down, the others were as docile as newborn calves."

Norm fished out a silver dollar and a half-dollar, handing them to Jack, who took the coins and dropped both into his vest pocket. "True, but I've seen cowhands be rough with folks. You handled it mighty well."

Jack shrugged. "You asked how long I've been carrying a badge. Let's just say for a long time." Jack changed the conversation's direction. "Thanks for the invite. I was hungry and enjoyed the conversation. You heading back to your farm?"

"Eventually. As soon as the store owners decide to brave the weather and open up, I'll pick up the supplies I need and head on back. Right now, I think I'll mosey over to the stables and check on my animals. My place ain't far west of here. If you're out that way, stop by. The coffee's hot, and I'll pick up a few pounds of sugar to take care of you."

Both men chuckled and turned their separate ways, Jack heading for the front desk, and Norm Caster to the hotel's front door.

The blast of cold air struck Jack as he reached the desk, and was gone. The old man sneezed, his bloodshot eyes watching Norm as he pulled the door closed and disappeared down the boardwalk.

"What can you tell me about Reno Flint?"

The question appeared to surprise Cap. He turned his attention from the disappearing farmer. Jack thought he caught a look of disapproval on the old man's face as he stared at Caster's back, but couldn't be sure.

"Flint? Not much to tell. He's a quiet feller, but I wouldn't want to cross him. Always wearing those dang black clothes. Why, he looks pert near like an undertaker except for those Colt .45s hangin' on his hips. Friendly enough. Runs a game in the Long Branch." He tilted his head, and his right eyebrow lifted at Jack. "Why you asking?"

"Law business."

Cap shook his head. "In my recollection, 'law business' don't usually work out too well for the feller on the wrong end."

Jack ignored the statement. "You say he deals at the Long Branch?"

"Yep."

"What hours?"

The clump of boots could be heard coming along the upstairs hallway.

"Why don't you ask him? Sounds like he's heading over there right now." Cap's face grew concerned. He leaned across the counter, and his voice dropped to a whisper. "Listen, Marshal. I don't know what's going on here, but there's a lot of folks in that there dining room. I sure wouldn't want any shooting. People might get hurt."

Jack's mind worked quickly. *I could end this right now and be on my way back to Grace before the sun sets, but Cap's right. There's a chance an innocent person could be hit, but the same possibility exists in the Long Branch.* He saw the man in black step from the hallway at the top of the stairs and begin his descent.

Flint was big, not as big as Bruiser, but bigger than Jack by at least twenty pounds and taller. Over his left arm, he carried a heavy black overcoat, and just like Jack had been told, a pair of .45-caliber Colt Peacemakers rode on his hips. He began his descent. His was a loose, confident gait, smooth and steady, no bouncing.

He wore a black brocade vest, black cravat, black shirt and trousers, with black boots and a slim-brimmed black Stetson. A tailored black frock coat enhanced the effect, with the coat's hem flipped back, uncovering the shiny Colts. Jack wasn't sure what type of wood the butts of the two Colts were made of, but suspected it to be ebony, which he was familiar with from Algiers. The gunfighter's right hand hung close to the Colt, and his eyes had followed Jack in his descent. Then suddenly shifted to the front door of the hotel.

At the instant they moved, the double doors crashed open. Jack spun, yelling at Cap, "Hit the floor!" His right hand snapped down to the .44-caliber Smith & Wesson American riding in its holster. Though Jack had worked endlessly on a two-handed draw, he knew his right hand was still a fraction faster, and he knew he would need every bit of speed he could muster, for the hulk who had crashed through the doors carried a devastating instrument of death in his hands.

Bruiser Bailey, his lips pulled back in an evil snarl, held a 10-gauge double-barrel shotgun. The muzzles looked large enough for a man to shove a fist down each. The hulking man's thick finger was rammed inside the trigger guard, and his snarl was turning into a confident grin as the butt of the shotgun neared his shoulder.

Jack knew he was about to be shot, but his body had gone into the cold, calculating response it always did when he entered a life-threatening conflict. Though his hands were moving so fast they were difficult to follow, in his mind, everything had slowed. The shotgun inexorably moved to Bruiser's shoulder while Jack's right hand lifted his own revolver. A thought flashed through his mind. *I hope Cap dropped out of the way because Bruiser'll have that thing loaded with triple-aught buckshot. At this range, it'll blow through me and take out anyone behind me.*

His draw continued, and he realized the turn was going to cost him. If he had been facing the door when Bruiser burst in, he would have had a chance, but the turn took too much time. His mind raced with thoughts of Grace and the boys.

Bruiser continued forward, raising the shotgun. He was close enough for Jack to see the wide finger tighten on the front trigger. *Just one moment more,* he thought as the muzzle of his Smith began to level.

A weapon blasted, and a hole appeared in Bruiser's chest. The shotgun's muzzle continued to travel up as his grin changed to a look of surprise and disbelief. He started to swing the muzzles from Jack and toward the stairs, but the 200-grain slug from Jack's Smith & Wesson slammed into Bruiser next to the bloody hole in his chest, driving him farther back and elevating the muzzles higher. They were pointed between Jack and the stairs when the first barrel discharged, filling the lobby with an earsplitting roar, smoke, and the acrid smell of black powder.

Jack fired again, this time taking aim with his revolver. Bruiser's head snapped back, a black hole appearing between and just above his thick eyebrows. Then it lurched to the side, another hole in his right temple, and he collapsed in a massive, bloody heap on the hotel floor. Jack's head whipped to the left in time to see Reno Flint slide his Colt back into its holster. Jack covered the door long enough to ensure Bruiser was alone, holstered his weapon, turned, and nodded to Flint. "Much obliged. If you hadn't fired, he would've punched my ticket."

A hand appeared at the counter edge. Cap pulled himself from the floor and hurried to the body stretched across the entrance to the hotel. He grabbed an arm of the dead man and pulled him out of the way of the doors. Next, he closed them, checking to make sure they would still latch. When they did, he turned to two men who had walked in from the back. "Don't just stand there. Get this idgit out of here. He's making a mess."

Jack shook his head. "Leave him."

Cap's head jerked up to Jack. "What? We need to get him out of here. I've got customers."

"Leave him until the marshal gets here. I'm sure he heard the shooting. He'll be showing up soon. Once he's seen him, he can authorize moving the body."

Cap looked at the blood on his floor. "Can I at least get some straw on this mess?"

"Sure you can. Just don't move him any more than you have to until the law gets here."

Cap looked back at the two men. "You heard him. Head over to the stables, and get some straw."

The two men didn't need a second prompting. They trotted across the lobby, past Cap, and disappeared through the doors as Marshal Taylor stepped in, weapon drawn.

Seeing Bruiser bloody and crumpled on the floor, he

holstered his weapon and looked at Flint, then Jack. The two men were now standing side by side. "What happened here?"

"Well, Marshal," Jack began, "Mr. Bailey settled his grudge. Thanks to Reno Flint, it didn't come out the way he'd planned."

"Anybody else hurt?"

Jack turned to look up at the room wall at the top of the stairs, where the load of buckshot had torn through the timbers. Fortunately, it was near the edge, joining the ceiling. "Unless there's an almighty tall man in that first room, Marshal, I'd say Mr. Bailey is the only injured party."

The lobby and the landing at the top of the stairs had filled with people. A well-dressed man standing in the entryway from the restaurant nodded at the dead man. "Bruiser was gonna kill the big fella at the counter. I saw it all. He burst in with that shotgun and was going to shoot the man in the back. Mr. Flint shot him a fraction before the stranger did. Bruiser never had a chance. The stranger was fast. He had his back to the door when Bruiser charged in, but he wouldn't have been fast enough. Mr. Flint saved the man from a back-shooter." The last words were spoken in disgust.

The marshal nodded to the speaker. "Thanks, Mr. Thompson. Later today, I'll stop by your shop with a statement you can sign."

Thompson nodded his agreement.

The hotel's front door opened again, and a small, round man stepped through the door. His bowler hat was held in place with a gray muffler pulled over the top, which was cinched under his chin and wrapped around his neck and face. After closing the door and unwrapping the muffler, he glanced at Bruiser and then at Marshal Taylor. "You through with him?"

"I am, Silas. You can take him."

The man nodded at the marshal and Cap and looked around the lobby. Then, in a clipped, businesslike tone, asked, "Anyone else need my service?"

"That's it," the marshal said.

Silas looked at Cap. "I'll have men down here shortly, Mr. Clements, to remove the body. I can remove the bloodstain for a small charge."

Cap gave a sharp shake of his head. "Not necessary, Silas. We'll take care of it."

"Very well." He nodded to the marshal, wrapped the muffler around his face, and stepped back when the two men arrived with arms full of straw, then hurried out the door.

While the commotion continued around the dead man, Marshal Taylor stepped over to Jack and Flint, who now stood side by side. He addressed Jack. "Do you think you would have beat him?"

Jack shook his head. "Not a chance. Those two fellas would've been spreading straw around my body and maybe Cap's if it hadn't been for this man."

The marshal turned to Flint. "Lucky you headed down the stairs when you did."

Flint shook his head. "I don't believe in luck, Marshal. Besides, it was mighty close. This fella's bullet hit Bruiser a split second after mine did, and that was with him having to make a turn." He looked at Jack with an appraising eye. "You were mighty fast."

Jack extended his hand to Flint. "Not fast enough. Since you saved my life, I guess I should introduce myself. Jack Sage."

4

Reno's gaze cooled as he took Jack's hand. "Maybe I shouldn't have been so quick to step in. I hear there's a U.S. Marshal following me by the name of Jack Sage. Would that be you?"

Jack released the man's grip, letting his hand drop comfortably to his side. "One and the same. We need to talk."

Marshal Taylor's head snapped back and forth, ending with Jack. "You need me to stay?"

Jack gave the marshal a wry grin. "No, Marshal, I think we'll be fine. I'll call you if I need you. Thanks."

The marshal turned, stopped for a moment to talk to Cap, then disappeared out the front door.

Outwardly relaxed, Flint said, "Marshal, I'm a late riser, and your little disagreement has kept me from my breakfast. The Long Branch provides me free meals. You mind if we talk there? That's where I was headed before Bruiser decided to interrupt." The gambler gave a small nod to his left. "It's just next door."

"Fine with me. I could go for a cup of coffee." He motioned to the door, and without a moment's hesitation, Flint stepped toward the door, nodding to Cap and the others. Jack followed. It was still cold, but the wind was decreasing a bit, and even without his overcoat, for the short distance, the cold was not so biting. Jack still held onto his hat, as did Flint. Only a few steps took them to the door of the Long Branch. Flint opened it, allowing Jack to precede him into the busy saloon.

It looked much the same as others Jack had entered. He estimated the bar length, which sat to the right, at around twenty-five feet. An aisle at the end of the bar led from the main area into a kitchen and probably outside. Directly across the aisle from the bar was an office.

The rest of the room comprised tables, and near the back sat a roulette table and a couple of faro tables. Against the far left wall, a set of stairs led to the second floor, where a landing ran the full width of the building. Six doors faced the landing.

Rooms, Jack thought. *It would be interesting to know if the girls who work here live in those rooms, or if they're used for other purposes.* Then he chuckled to himself. *Always thinking like a lawman.*

"This way," Flint said, and turned left to a table near the foot of the stairs and against the wall.

Jack, without a word, followed the gunman to the table and watched him pick the chair nearest the wall. Jack chose the one next to him facing the stairs, pulled it out, and lowered himself. He took time to examine the people in the saloon. He wasn't worried about Flint. Jack knew men, and this man was no backshooter. If he fought Jack, it would be face-to-face. There would be no subterfuge.

The bartender was like many of the men who tended bar in the west, big, with a nose that had been broken several times, and scars covering his knuckles. Jack figured him for a tough man in a fight and willing to fight when necessary.

Several women floated between tables, laughing and running their hands over the backs and shoulders of the patrons. Their laughter and touches were returned with grins and comments, which brought more laughter. Then, of course, the incessant piano banged away. If there was any one reason Jack hated to go into a saloon, besides not being much of a drinker, it was the ear-torturing banging of the pianos.

When he was a young boy, his mother had paid for piano lessons for him. She did not know that her sweet young son couldn't carry a tune in a bucket and not only disliked music, but found it almost painful to his ears. For some strange reason he could never explain, the piano's sound tortured his ears more than any other instrument. When he could take it no longer, he explained to his disappointed mother how music hurt his ears. After hearing his explanation, she allowed him to do something unheard of in the Sage family—quit.

An attractive young redhead with deep blue eyes and a low-cut bodice hurried to their table. She flashed a smile at Jack, but he could see her obvious destination was Reno Flint. She rushed to his side and gave his neck a long squeeze. "Hi, honey. I'm glad you're alright after all that shooting next door. I've missed you. Would you like your regular breakfast?"

Flint patted the girl's slim arm, lifted her hand, and kissed it gently. "That would be fine." He nodded to Jack. "This is Linda. She's a mighty sweet girl. Linda, this is Jack."

Linda's smile grew larger. "Hi, Jack. What can I get you?"

"Ma'am, I'd appreciate a hot cup of coffee, about two-thirds full, and milk and sugar."

"Wouldn't you like something stronger? It may be early in the day, but that don't mean nothing."

"No, ma'am, I reckon coffee would be fine."

She dipped her head beneath Flint's hat and gave him a kiss on the cheek. "Alright, baby, I'll be right back."

She did a swishing turn toward the kitchen, and Flint swatted her on the bottom. "Bring me a deck of cards, too." She laughed, waved, and hurried across the room.

Reno watched her depart and turned to say something to Jack.

Before he could begin, a scruffy-looking man wearing a stained and beat-up hat stepped up to the table. "This table open, Flint?"

Reno's demeanor changed. The grin vanished, replaced by a hard-set jaw. His gray eyes were as hard as his last name. He stared at the intruder. "It'll never be open for you, Cochran. You best haul your freight."

"Don't talk to me like that, Flint, or I'll tell Besson. He'll fire you on the spot."

Reno pushed back from the table, his chair scraping across the rough-hewn floor. He let his right hand rest on his leg. "Last word, Cochran. Hit the door."

The man waited a moment. His face reddened as he considered his next move. Then his lips curled into a sneer. "I ain't leavin', and our business ain't finished." He spun toward the bar, uttering something inaudible under his breath.

Reno slid himself back to the table and watched Linda work her way toward them with the deck of cards and Jack's coffee. She dodged occupied tables and grasping hands, laughing and joking with the men while she balanced a tray held high. He pulled his eyes from the sensuous woman and turned to Jack. "Cochran owns a little two-by-twice spread down the river. He was in here and lost big a few nights ago. Blamed me because I was dealing. He let his mouth run away with him. It was a question of killing him or throwing him out."

Jack watched Cochran make his way to the bar and slam his hand on the polished surface. "He's spoiling for a fight. You're not through with him."

"Yeah, I know."

Jack heard the resignation in Reno's voice. They both knew Cochran was working himself up to a gunfight. He watched the rancher throw a drink back and demand another. "The way he's drinking, you won't have long to wait."

Before Reno could respond, Linda reached their table with the cards and coffee. She placed the cards gently into the gambler's big hand, her fingers slipping lightly over his. Turning to Jack, Linda placed coffee, cream, and sugar in front of him, flashed another wide smile at Reno, and swished her way back through the tables.

This time, Reno turned serious gray eyes on Jack. "So, Marshal Sage, what have I done to get a U.S. Marshal on my trail?"

Jack had added sugar to his coffee and now poured enough cream into the cup to bring the mixture almost to the rim. Stirring cautiously until he was satisfied, he laid the spoon on the side of the saucer and took a long sip. "Ahh, mighty good." He reached into the inside pocket of his coat, pulled out the warrant, and handed it to Flint.

The gambler's lips pursed, and his forehead wrinkled as he took the warrant, opened it, and began to read.

While Flint read, Jack kept watch on Cochran. The man had already thrown down several drinks in rapid succession. The last one, he tossed back and slammed the empty glass onto the bar with finality. Turning, he pulled his weapon, allowing his arm to hang toward the floor, and started for Jack and Flint's table. The drunk man, for Jack had seen him stumble, quickly covered half the distance from the bar.

That's enough, Jack thought. He stood and, loud enough to be heard over the din, said, "I'm a United States Marshal. Holster that sixgun."

Cochran stopped, the revolver still hanging at his side.

Jack watched the gunman. He could almost see this new piece of information laboring to make its way through the fog of drink and into the man's pickled brain. *The last thing I want to do is try to reason with an armed drunk,* Jack thought.

Flint began to stand. With his left hand, Jack grabbed the man's shoulder and shoved him back into his chair. "Stay down."

"This is my fight, Sage!"

"No, it isn't. I'm here, and I'm the law. There'll be no gunplay unless I make it."

The word gunplay cut its way through the racket like a trapper's skinning knife. The incessant clanging of the piano stopped, and chairs scraped. Patrons, some stumbling, scattered like a covey of quail from the line of fire. The drunken man swayed from side to side.

Disbelievingly, he asked, "You a real marshal?"

"I am. I'm going to pull my coat back so you can see my badge." Jack raised his left hand, grasped his coat at the second button, and pulled it back far enough to expose the badge secured to his vest.

Cochran squinted, staring at the glinting star. "And you're protecting that card sharp?"

Jack shook his head. "No, I'm protecting you. He'd kill you before you could get your weapon leveled. Have you ever seen him draw?"

The man stared at Jack and slowly shook his head.

"He's the fastest draw I know besides me."

Jack could see reason returning through the fog of drink. A bead of sweat broke out on Cochran's forehead, ran into his eyebrow, and clung there like a desperate man clinging to a cliff. His eyes shifted from Jack's face to the edge of his coat, flipped back, exposing his Smith & Wesson .44.

"Mr. Cochran, in this business, I can't take the chance of attempting to wing a person when I fire. I shoot to kill so I can survive. There's been other men who thought they were faster. They're no longer on this earth. I don't want to kill you, and I don't want you to fire that hogleg into this crowd. Look around you. These are your friends and neighbors. I know it's not your intention to put any of your lead into these folks. Be smart, and holster that sixgun."

Cochran's eyes cut to Reno and back to Jack. He took a deep breath, gave a long sigh, and slowly eased the weapon toward his holster.

Though Jack's hand hung loose at his side, his body was poised and ready. "Easy now. Keep the muzzle pointed down. Lift it straight up, and drop it into your holster, then raise both hands."

The would-be gunfighter had turned pale. He followed Jack's directions, then stretched both hands like he was trying to touch the ceiling. Jack stepped quickly around the table, reached for Cochran, and was unfastening his gunbelt when the man spoke, his voice shaky. Nodding at Flint, he asked, "Is he really that fast?"

With the gunbelt removed, Jack wrapped the belt around the holster. "You would've been dead before that hogleg reached level. You've made a smart decision. Now, let's head over to the marshal's office."

Cochran had been staring at Flint. At the mention of the marshal, he looked up at Jack. "I'm going to jail?"

Jack's forehead wrinkled, and his eyes narrowed. He moved his face close to the drunk's. "You just tried to kill a man. What do you expect?"

Flint called, "You going to leave me here?" He waved the warrant.

"I found you this time. If you run, I'll find you again. Meet me in the hotel in an hour."

"I'll be deep in a game by then."

"We need to talk. Don't make me chase you."

Flint stiffened. "I wasn't running. I was just moving on." He paused, staring at Jack's hard gray eyes. "Alright, I'll be there."

Jack nodded. He didn't want to drag Cochran back to the table to get the warrant. *I'll trust him and see what happens,* he thought. "Bring the warrant."

The piano and noise had begun again. Except for the cold awaiting him outside, Jack was more than ready to be out of the Long Branch.

~

IT WAS STILL COLD, especially without his overcoat. Jack opened the door and stepped inside the Harbor Hotel. In the lobby's corner, next to the dining room wall, sat two large, well-padded cowhide-covered chairs with wide wooden arms. Reno Flint occupied one. The gambler's expression gave no emotion away. He sat with legs crossed at the knee, one black boot swinging slowly forward and back, like a man of leisure.

Reno's eyes locked on him the moment he stepped through the door, and tracked him like a cougar eyeing its prey. "You took your own sweet time."

"It took longer than I thought to explain to Marshal Taylor about Cochran."

"Will he be held over for trial?"

Jack shook his head. "I don't think so. He's still sobering up. We had to stop on the way to the jail. He started shaking and puked. I'd lay odds he's thankful he didn't try you. You won't have any more problems from him."

The chair groaned as Jack lowered himself into it. "You ready for a trip?"

"I'm not going back to Independence, Marshal."

Jack allowed his weight to sink into the chair's thick padded back. "You remember killing that young fella in Independence." It wasn't a question.

"Of course I do. Don't you remember every man you've killed?"

Jack's mind went to a dusty street in Texas and a young ex-ranger who had been fired from the rangers for being too quick with his sixgun. He had goaded several other men into gunfights and had killed them, and his so-called friends had convinced him he was the fastest man alive, and he should settle his grudge with Sage. *Yeah,* Jack thought, *I remember them all.* After the smoke cleared, Jack had mounted Smokey and headed west, passing the young fella dying in the dusty street. He nodded. "I remember them all, Reno, but you should have let this one walk away."

Reno uncrossed his legs, and leaned toward Jack, his hands gripping the thick wooden arms of the chair. "That's a laugh. I *tried* to walk away, but the kid wouldn't let me. He said if I showed him my back, he'd put a bullet in it. What would you have done?"

"Tell me what happened."

"Why is this so important? I hated to shoot the kid, but he forced my hand. There were plenty of witnesses around. I remember them swearing to the sheriff that I was prodded into it and had no choice. Shoot, Marshal, if he'd been innocent, that sheriff would have arrested me, or there would be wanted posters everywhere. Have you seen any?"

Jack shook his head, his eyes fixed on Flint. "No, I haven't, but I asked you to tell me what happened." Jack held out his hand. "I'll take that warrant back."

The gambler pulled the folded paper from inside his vest, handed it to Jack, and collapsed into his chair. "Alright. I don't much like talking about it, but here goes. We'd been playing poker, and the kid was good. He started out taking my money, but, unfortunately for him, he had a major tell. When he had a good hand, he invariably licked his lips. After I caught that, I cleaned him out. He wanted to keep playing with markers. I told him he played a good game, but it was time for him to take a break, and I only played for cash."

Reno removed the black, narrow-brimmed, flat-crowned Stetson, combed his fingers through thick black hair, put the hat back on, and shook his head. "He got mad, but he finally left. The game continued, and I forgot all about him. Several hours passed. It was getting late, and I was tired, so I was preparing to step out of the game. Just as I slid my chair back, in he stomps, madder than a poked rattler. He marches within ten feet of the table and calls me a card sharp and a cheater, plus a few other choice names.

"Several of the other folks who knew me tried to reassure the kid I wasn't a cheater, that the cards had just turned against him, but he wasn't buying it. Even the barkeep tried to step in and persuade him he was making a mistake. The kid turned on him, accusing him of being in on the cheating and telling him he'd put a bullet through his gullet if he didn't shut up. I let him blow off steam, hoping he'd calm down, but he just seemed to get madder. That's when I tried to walk out of there. I had already picked up my earnings. Like I said, I was ready to call it a night.

"Suddenly he quit talking and, with no warning, drew. The kid was faster than most cowhands." Reno stopped, his gray eyes staring out the window at the now bustling street.

Jack waited, saying nothing. He knew Flint was playing the action over in his mind. After a brief period, his eyes focused on Jack for a second, then glanced down at his well-manicured nails before he continued.

"What can I say, Marshal? I shot the kid. There was no time to try to wing him. He was too fast. I shot him right through the heart. He was dead before he hit the floor. He was a good kid before he let his anger take over, around twenty-five, maybe a little less, maybe more. However old he was, he isn't going to get any older." The hardened gambler in black shook his head. "It was a fair fight, but fair doesn't give him his life back. He's not the first I've killed, and I doubt he'll be the last, but their faces stay with you."

Flint took a deep breath, slowly let it out, and refocused on Jack. "That's it. That's the whole story other than the sheriff suggesting I move on, which I did." He shook his head again. "I really hated to leave Independence. It was a profitable place." He shrugged. "Oh well, moving on goes with the territory, and I have to admit, I still like discovering what's on the other side of the next hill. I rode the cushions here, stopped several times along the way to test the water, and here I am."

Grasping the arms of the chair, Flint leaned toward Jack again. "So what's the big problem? Why the federal warrant? And why is it signed by the president? It was just another shootout in a two-bit town."

5

Jack shook his head. "Not quite."

Flint's countenance darkened. His forehead wrinkled, eyebrows drew together, and lips tightened. "I told you what happened. It was a fair fight. You can talk to anyone there. Those folks will tell you exactly what I told you. The kid drew. I had no other choice."

Jack held up the warrant. "You saw who signed this."

"I saw his name. Why's he after me? What did I ever do to *him*?"

The question hung in the air between them. Jack shoved the warrant back inside his coat pocket and gazed out the window, thoughts racing through his mind. *Reno Flint strikes me as an honest man. I don't agree with his lifestyle, but I'm growing to trust him. If he's right and witnesses swore to his being justified in the shooting, why would the president sign this warrant?* He turned back to the gambler. "As far as I know, you haven't done anything to the president. Unfortunately for you, the man you killed was Sean Harris Jr., the son of Senator Sean Harris from Pennsylvania, who is the president's good friend."

A curse escaped Reno's lips. "Why couldn't that kid take his losses and leave me be?" Then hard gray eyes locked on Jack. "I'm not going back to Independence, Marshal. That senator will stack the deck. There's not a snowball's chance I'd get a fair trial. You know that."

Jack shook his head. "Be reasonable. We can grab a train and be there in a day's time. I'll talk to the sheriff and a few of the witnesses, get a message off to the president, and this thing will be behind you. You don't want a federal warrant hanging over your head. There won't just be marshals after you. They'll send out the whole blasted army. To make it worse, the senator could put a bounty on you, and you'd have bounty hunters sniffing out your trail no matter where you tried to hide. You'd be looking over your shoulder constantly until you're caught or killed. Come back with me now, and we can get this mistake settled. You'll be free of any accusations and can go on living your life. Keep your guns. We'll stay in whatever hotel you want, no jails. Let's get this straightened out as soon as possible."

Jack watched the gunman mull over the offer. *What am I doing?* Jack thought. *I just met this fella. Granted, he saved my life, but what do I know about him? What I know is how fouled up the courts can get, especially with a United States senator applying pressure. I also know he could've run when I left him in the Long Branch. Come on, Flint, give it a chance.* And then the thought he'd been trying to keep out of his mind pushed its way in. *I don't want to have to kill you.*

Reno stared into Jack's eyes. It was as if he were trying to discern truth from fiction. "Are you telling me the truth, Marshal? This is my life we're talking about."

Jack met his stare with a frank, honest gaze of his own, refusing to take offense at the suggestion he was lying. "Listen, Reno, you don't know me, but I don't lie. If it went down like you said, and I have no reason to doubt you, I can verify the events of your story. I won't let anyone harm you, not a senator or even a president. You saved my life, and for some crazy reason, I trust you. It's time for you to trust me."

Reno continued to watch him. "The first I heard about you was the story in newspapers all over the country about your cleaning up that little town in Texas, Cherry something. After that, tales of you have drifted around. None of them mentioned anything about you other than you being a straight shooter, but you're asking a lot of me."

Jack said nothing.

"I don't have to give up my guns?"

"Nope."

Reno Flint waited, eyes steady on Jack. At last, he began to nod. "Alright, Marshal. I don't want to be hiding in a coyote's den for the rest of my life. I'll go back with you." His eyes narrowed, and small wrinkles bunched along his forehead. "But I promise you, I'm not going to jail for an honest shoot. If I smell a rat, at any time, I'm leaving, and I'll shoot any man who tries to stop me, including you."

Jack felt the threat and knew it for the weight it carried. He extended his hand. "Good, hopefully it won't come to that."

Reno's face still showed worry as he took Jack's hand. "I hope not, Marshal, for I mean what I say."

"So do I. You can bank on that."

Reno nodded. "Knowing you're a man of your word is the only reason I'm going back with you. When do we leave?"

Jack stood. "As soon as we can catch a train. Let's get this over with."

~

THE TRAIN PULLED INTO INDEPENDENCE, Missouri, in the early afternoon of a cold, dreary day. Jack had a window seat and saw Carter Schofield standing on the station's platform. He was among folks waiting to greet friends, business associates, and loved ones.

What is Carter doing here? Jack thought.

Reno, who had been looking past Jack, saw the man he was looking at and his reaction. "Is there trouble, Jack?"

Jack examined the platform from end to end. Nothing, no deputies, no troops. He was puzzled that Carter was awaiting him here in Independence. *At least he's by himself,* Jack thought, then turned to Reno. "I don't think so. The man on the platform is my liaison with the president. His being here is unexpected, but I don't see it as a problem."

The train's wheels screeched against the rails when the engineer braked the train to a stop, perfectly aligned with the platform. It gave one final jerk, the weight of the cars eliciting a metallic crunch, after which the passengers quickly stood, eager to get off the train and meet those who were waiting for them. Jack sat tight. He wanted to allow the civilians to disembark and safely clear the train. Jack didn't expect trouble from Carter, but his being here could indicate a problem. He hoped not.

The conductor walked slowly through the train, examining each empty seat as he passed. Nearing the two men, he smiled. "Independence, gentlemen, end of the line."

Jack nodded, stood, and stepped into the aisle. Flint followed suit, motioning for Jack to go ahead. One side of Jack's mouth moved up slightly. "Not very trusting."

Flint gave him the same look. "I may be a gambler, Marshal, but I like to think I'm not a stupid one." His grin disappeared, replaced by concern and apprehension. "I saw your face. You didn't look too pleased when you spotted your, what did you call him, liaison? I know you, but I don't know how trustworthy he is."

Jack nodded and proceeded down the aisle to the exit. Most of the people had greeted those awaiting them and were now drifting away from the station. From the train step, Jack placed his foot on the stool that had been positioned at the bottom of the stairs for the passengers.

Carter started forward, saw Reno, paused a step, and continued, a faint smile of satisfaction on his face. Reaching Jack, he extended his hand, shaking Jack's enthusiastically until he saw Reno Flint wasn't in irons but was armed, both of his .45-caliber Colt Peacemakers peeking out from under his open overcoat. He demanded of Jack, "Why is this man armed?"

Jack, towering over Carter, replied in a calm but firm voice, "It's good to see you, too, Carter. I'd like you to meet Reno Flint. He saved my life."

Surprised, Carter looked first at Flint and then back to Jack, his voice beginning to rise. "What do you mean, saved your life?"

Flint remained silent.

"Just what I said. The man saved my life yesterday morning in Dodge City."

Carter, confused and off balance but desiring answers rather than an altercation in public, stared up at Jack. "What is the meaning of this? This man killed Senator Harris's son. I want an answer. Why is he still armed?"

Jack, never a patient man, felt tingling in his scalp, the first sign of creeping anger. "We don't have to air it out here, Carter. We're hungry. Why don't we find a decent place and have a bite to eat?"

Carter stepped forward, unused to not having his questions answered immediately. His face reddening, and voice rising, he drove a forefinger into Jack's chest. "I asked you a question, Marshal. You work for me. I expect an answer right now."

Several people on the train platform had stopped and were now watching this smaller man raising his voice to two men hulking over him. Reno Flint smiled and nodded to them.

Jack felt the same cool wave wash over him that engulfed him just before a fight. He leaned forward and down so the brim of his hat slid over the top of Carter's, stopping at the crown. His eyes were only four inches away from his liaison's. He had taken a deep breath on the way down, and now his gray eyes were calmer than they were seconds before, but he was still riled. "Carter, the last time you let your temper get away from you, I threw this badge at your feet. You managed to talk me into taking it back. If I do it again, I'll be done. Now cool yourself and think about what you're doing. Look around. Folks are staring at you."

Jack raised up and glanced at Flint. "You have any problem going to the sheriff's office first? That way, he can tell Carter here what happened."

Flint jerked back. "You're not pulling a trick on me now, are you?"

Jack hadn't even considered the line of thought Flint took. "No, man. I'm just thinking if we can clear the air, then I can talk to Schofield here and get both of us back on our way to Dodge City on the next train."

Flint looked at Carter Schofield, who so far had not uttered a word to him. Then he looked at Jack. He rubbed his chin and thought for a moment. "Well, alright. I've trusted you this far. Let's play this hand to the end."

"Good." Jack turned to Carter. "Is that alright with you?"

Carter's face was still red, and he looked like he had more to say, but only nodded.

"Let's go. I want to get this done and hit the feedbag. I'm hungry." Jack, with Carter Schofield, the representative of the president of the United States on one side, and Reno Flint, the killer of Sean Harris Jr. on the other, headed for the sheriff's office.

It was near the train station. Nothing was said during the short journey. Jack ignored the still steaming Schofield. He had stolen another glance at the man, and it seemed he was getting angrier with each step they took. Reaching the sheriff's office, Jack stepped up to the door, pulled the latch, and walked in. Flint followed, and Carter Schofield brought up the rear.

The sheriff's potbelly stove was pumping out heat. A coffeepot sat on the side, steaming. Two deputies relaxed in straight-backed chairs, drinking coffee, and the sheriff was behind his desk, his feet resting on a stack of wanted posters. He, too, sipped on a cup of coffee. When he saw Reno Flint, a frown drifted across his face, and he set his cup down. "Reno, boy, I'm glad to see you're in good health, but I distinctly remember asking you to mosey on out of here."

"I'm not back because I want to be, Sheriff." He looked at Jack, but before Jack could respond, Carter Schofield spoke up.

"Sheriff, I want you to arrest this man for the murder of Sean Harris Jr."

Jack stepped past Flint, confronting Schofield. "Now just wait a minute, Carter."

Schofield raised his hand to jab Jack in the chest again, but this time Jack caught the smaller man's wrist in a big hand and clenched tight. Not so tight anything could be broken, but tight enough to let Schofield know he was making a big mistake. "What's the matter with you, Carter? I told you not to do that."

Still holding Carter's wrist, Jack glanced at the sheriff. "Sorry to barge in on you, Sheriff. I'm Jack Sage, U.S. Marshal, and this fella is Carter Schofield, agent for President Grant."

The sheriff put his cup down and stood, his frown growing deeper. When the sheriff rose, so did the two deputies, still gripping their cups but confused by the disturbance.

Carter Schofield attempted to twist his wrist from Jack's grip, with no luck. He spoke through a grimace, trying unsuccessfully to hide the pain. "Turn me loose, Sage, or I swear, you'll never work for the president again."

Jack, turning back from the sheriff, felt like either cinching down on the wrist or slapping Schofield. *What's wrong with him?* he thought, but, exasperated, relaxed his grip. "Settle down, Carter. Let's get this worked out, and then I'll gladly give you this badge."

When Jack relaxed his grip, Carter Schofield jerked his hand away and began rubbing his wrist. He turned to the sheriff. "Sheriff, I told you I want Reno Flint arrested. I told you, he murdered—"

The sheriff's face was grim. "Mr. Schofield, or whatever your name is, Reno Flint ain't guilty of anything in this town. He defended himself against a feller who tried to kill him, but it sure weren't murder. Now, like Marshal Sage here said, you need to calm down and tell me what this is all about."

Jack felt a shock course through his body like he'd been hit by lightning. He knew Carter carried a shoulder holster under his coat on his left side, but he'd never seen the man use it. He was also aware Carter had little fear of injury or even death. His duties as a spy during the war had hardened him. The man wasn't afraid of conflict, and now Carter's right hand was driving under his coat toward his shoulder holster.

Jack glanced back at Reno Flint, who had registered the move and was responding in kind, his right hand flashing down to his Colt. *No!* his mind screamed. *This can't be happening. I've got to protect Carter no matter how crazy he's acting.* Jack drew.

Throughout all the time of his draw, his mind raced. *Don't draw, Reno. Don't do it.*

In a blur, Reno's Peacemaker rose from his holster.

Carter's wrist began to emerge from behind his coat.

Jack's Smith & Wesson was rising from its holster, and the sheriff was yelling, "Nooo!"

With his big left hand, Jack shoved Carter with all the force he could muster, slamming him against the wall.

Carter's hand jerked from under his coat, and Reno fired. The bullet clipped the edge of Carter's arm, wool and blood flying across the room.

Jack, his duty clear to protect Carter Schofield, was only a split second behind Flint, and his bullet struck where it was aimed, driving shards of the third button of Reno's overcoat deep into his chest. The crash of guns in the sheriff's office was deafening, the blasts sounding as one.

Reno staggered, his back striking the bars of the jail. He gaped at the white paper clutched in Schofield's right hand and slowly slid down the bars to the floor.

Jack dashed to the gambler's side, dropped to his knees, and yelled at the man, "Why did you draw, Reno?"

Reno Flint gasped, blood beginning to trickle from the edge of his mouth. He coughed and flashed Jack a lopsided grin. "I knew I shouldn't have come back to Independence."

In the background, Jack heard the sheriff yell to one of the deputies, "Get the doc!"

The grin disappeared. "I made a mistake, Jack." A fit of coughing overcame him, and his face began to lose its deep tan, turning pale, almost pasty. "I thought he was going for a gun."

Jack shook his head. "I'm sorry. The Lord knows I'm sorry, Reno."

The gambler's grin was weaker, and his head nodded, his chin almost reaching his chest. "Guess I'll be able to find out for sure what He knows, pretty quick."

This can't be happening, Jack thought. *This man saved my life, and I just killed him.*

From somewhere Reno gathered enough strength. He had gently laid his weapon on the floor, and now he reached up with a big hand and gripped Jack's shoulder. His voice was only a whisper. "Listen, Jack. I don't blame you. If we'd had more time, we would've been great friends. You did what you had to do. I'm the one who made the mis . . ." His voice tapered off into a long sigh. His hand dropped to his lap, and Reno Flint was dead.

Jack remained kneeling next to the gambler. He stared, through misty gray eyes, at the big man and realized his ears were ringing from the gunfire, like they had yesterday when Reno had saved his life. The same familiar smell of burned gunpowder filled the office. It was only yesterday, and it was yesterday he had talked him into coming to Independence. Now he'd killed him. Shot him dead.

"Marshal Sage?"

Jack felt the sheriff's hand on his shoulder. He blinked his eyes to free them of the mist, realizing he still held the Smith & Wesson in his right hand. Nodding, he dropped the weapon into its holster and stood.

His empty right hand slipped under his coat to his vest, and he removed the United States Marshal badge. Turning, his eyes searched for Carter Schofield. The man had regained his feet from where he had been propelled against the wall by Jack's shove. He still gripped the paper in his hand as blood ran down his wrist and fingers and dripped from the document.

Silently, Jack strode to his liaison, grabbed the hand holding the paper, and thrust the badge into it. His voice was low and cold. "How could you be so stupid?" He turned to the sheriff. "Sheriff . . . I didn't get your name."

"Hank, Hank Tyson."

"Sheriff Tyson, I'm mighty sorry about this."

The sheriff shook his head. "It happened too quick for everybody." He nodded toward Schofield. "I was just like Reno. I thought that feller Schofield was going for a gun. In fact, I had mine half drawn, but I hate to say it, I didn't know who to shoot. You did what was right. You had no other choice."

Jack shook his head. "Reno Flint was a good man. He was only defending himself against what he saw as a threat."

"Yeah. A bad situation all around. I've heard of you, man. You've done a lot of good in this country. You ain't really quitting?"

Jack gave a long sigh. "Sheriff Tyson, you have witnessed my last official killing. I'm done. When defending the law means killing a man who just saved your life, it's time to hang up the badge. In fact, I think it's way past time. Do you need me for the inquest?"

"Shoot no, Marshal. We've got four witnesses, and three of 'em are wearing badges. There weren't nothin' else you could've done. You're free to go."

"Jack?"

Jack Sage turned to see Carter behind him, the doctor bandaging the man's arm. He ignored him. Pulling his coat tight, he nodded to the deputies and stepped through the door into the cold breeze. The fresh air blew over him, cleansing, revitalizing, taking the smell of death away. Jack turned for the train station.

His mind filled with thoughts. *I wish I'd brought my animals with me. The last thing I want to do is go back to Dodge City and tell those folks what happened to Reno, especially that poor girl, Linda. Even so, I need to go there before I can return to where I belong. The woman and boys who love me are waiting. I hope there's a train headed there this evening.*

He continued toward the station.

6

Jack pulled up at the treeline of Fort Smith. Here it was, early February, and it felt like spring. He had shucked his coat and was down to his vest. Birds were singing, dogs barking, and the town was humming. Wagons crowded in at the front of the Far West Emporium, and Jack could see the owner, Nathan Gideon, assisting in loading. It was a thriving business and a bustling town, and there was one green-eyed citizen he was especially eager to see.

Jack's concerns drifted through his thoughts. *I hope she's eager to see me after all this time. Shoot, she may have already forgotten about me.* Jack bumped Smokey in the flanks, and with Pepper, Thunder, and his mule, Stonewall, in trail, they rode into town. He had barely made it into the busy town when he heard a call. "Jack, you old son of a gun, hold up there." He'd recognize that voice anywhere. It was none other than U.S. Deputy Marshal Buck Walker. He pulled up, and Buck strode into the street, extending his gloved hand.

"Howdy, Jack. We didn't expect you back so soon." The deputy gave an obvious glance at the empty spot on his vest. "Heard you told 'em to put that badge where the sun don't shine. You doing alright?"

Jack stopped in the middle of the street and took Buck's hand. "How are you, Buck? Let's just say I resigned, alright?"

Buck examined Jack's face. "Why shore, Jack. That's fine with me. It's good to have you back. Don't rightly know if you've heard or not, but Barrett Clagg got himself all healed up and escaped. Just walked out of the prison infirmary dressed as a guard. They found the missing guard. It took a while. He was stuffed in a locker, his throat slashed. Anyway, Barrett's out and about. Thought you'd like to know."

Jack was itching to see Grace and the boys. He kept looking along the boardwalks and street, thinking he might spot them.

An impish grin slipped across Buck's face. "Boys are in school today, Jack, and it's getting nigh on to dinnertime. In fact, I'm headin' over there in a few minutes. I imagine Gracie's working hard in the kitchen about now."

Jack looked down at his friend with feigned surprise. "What? Oh, yeah, I bet you're right."

Buck stepped back from Jack's big horse, Smokey. "Git on out of here, Jack. You're worse than a lovestruck calf. She'll be thrilled to see you. We're all getting tired of her talking about you around the table."

Jack's eyes narrowed, and his eyebrows pulled close together. "Buck, don't make me get down off this horse and whip you up and down this street."

Buck laughed. "You're gettin' too old, Jack. You couldn't catch me." The deputy grew serious. "It's good to see you back here and safe. In all seriousness, she's been worried about you."

Jack touched his finger to the brim of his Stetson. "Thanks, Buck. Good to see you, too." He clucked at Smokey, and they were on their way. He had to guide his entourage around several wagons until reaching Winthrop's Stables. In a chair, front legs off the ground, and leaning against a section of the wall, sat Pauly

Winthrop. His hat was pulled low over his eyes while he baked in the warm rays of the sun.

Jack pulled Smokey to a stop. "Pauly, you think I could disturb your reverie to persuade you to take care of my horses this fine afternoon?"

The big man, still leaning against the wall in his chair, pushed his hat back with one finger and eyed Jack. "You know, Jack, it could be considered unfriendly to disturb a poor man soaking his old bones in the sun."

"You'll get no sympathy from me. I just finished what amounted to a round trip to Dodge City. I think my rear is growing to this saddle. All I want to do is stretch my legs and eat something other than jerky and beans."

Pauly let the front of his chair drop to the ground, stretched his long arms, and yawned. "Dang, Jack, I swear you are a hard man. Come on in, and let's see if we can find a place for those fine animals. I'm sure *they* need to rest up." He returned the chair to its previous position against the wall and, while he was talking, waved Jack to follow him, stepping inside the wide-open entrance into the stable.

Inside, Jack swung to the ground and held onto the saddle for a moment. The old gunshot wound in his right thigh still bothered him when he was in the saddle for an extended period. His leg would stiffen and stay that way until he could walk it off.

Pauly missed nothing. "Stiff? That was a long ride."

"Yeah, old bullet wound. Bothers me occasionally." He drew the leg up several times, then walked around, stretching. Satisfied, he stepped back to Smokey. "Any particular stall?"

Pauly shook his head. "Same place works fine for me. I know Stonewall and Smokey are big buds."

Jack led the big grulla, Smokey, and his mule, Stonewall, to the double stall. It seemed like they had been with him forever, and the two animals had developed a genuine friendship. He had picked them both up in Mexico years ago. The grulla, called by some a gray dun, was gray with a white face and black markings. Gray stripes set off his four black stockings. Both animals were strong and dependable. Jack did his best to take care of them and his other two horses, Pepper and Thunder.

He removed the packs from Stonewall, then stripped the packsaddle and remaining tack, carrying all of it to the tack room. Next, he went to work on Smokey, relieving him of all the gear he was carrying.

Pauly was carrying feed to the four troughs, but stopped. "Grab what you need and leave the rest. I'll take care of it. You've had a long, hard trip. Sorry about what happened, but I know someone will be happy to see you. Don't keep her waiting."

Jack stopped. "Does everyone know about Independence?"

Pauly nodded. "Mostly. Hate to see you hang up that badge. Can't say I've ever met a lawman like you."

Jack pulled his rifle from the boot and picked up his saddlebags. "Thanks, Pauly."

The big liveryman gave a single nod and began working on Pepper. Jack reached into his vest pocket to pay the man.

Pauly saw him and shook his head. "No need, Jack. You go on and see Gracie and those boys. You're all they talk about. Drop back by and take care of that when you've got a spare minute."

"Thanks, Pauly. I'll be back over this afternoon. Those horse cookies are in the almost empty pack from Stonewall."

Pauly stopped and raised up from Pepper's flank. "Doggone it, Jack. I'm makin' 'em now. I'll give one to each animal. Now you go on and git. Go see that girl."

Grinning, Jack shook his head. "Yes, sir."

He could feel the butterflies start immediately when he stepped out of the livery. It had been months since he had ridden out of here with the taste of Grace's lips on his. *It's good to hear she's still talking about me,* he thought. *Maybe she still misses me. She's on my mind all the time.*

A number of men approached Ma's Bed and Eats boardinghouse. *Definitely dinnertime,* Jack thought. *It looks like half the businessmen in town are making their way here, and some of the women. That's a lot more people than they could've fed before.*

Reaching the door, he leaned over to grasp the knob, and there was a shout behind him and the sound of running feet. He turned just in time to keep from being bowled over by two boys who had launched themselves well before reaching the boardwalk. They both yelled in unison, "Marshal Sage! You're home."

Jack grasped a boy in each arm, squeezed, and lifted them from the ground. "It's good to see you boys. Look at you. I've only been gone a month or two, and you must've grown two feet. What's your ma been feeding you?"

Billy, the oldest at twelve, pushed against his arm to get down. "Aww, you're pulling our legs. We ain't grown two feet. Anyway, you've been gone longer than two months." He grinned at Jack. "But we've been working mighty hard, making money." He turned to Elijah. "Ain't that right, Eli?"

When Jack lowered the younger Elijah to the boardwalk, the boy was nodding his head enthusiastically. "We sure have." His face grew solemn. "Marshal, we're really glad you're back. We heard a fella almost backshot you."

"Boys, I'm fine, and I'm glad to see you both. Now, aren't you two supposed to be helping your ma with the serving?"

Dramatically, Billy slapped his forehead, almost knocking his hat off. "Oh my goodness, yes. Ma will kill us. Come on in, Marshal. She'll be mighty happy to see you. She talks about you all the time."

Jack grinned. "She does, huh?"

Billy grabbed the door handle and pushed the door open, grinning back at Jack and wiggling his eyebrows. "She sure does."

Elijah raced in behind his brother, yelling as he passed Jack, "She sure does!"

He heard Grace from the kitchen call, "Where have you boys been? Get in here."

Laughing to himself, he stepped through the front door. There were two more tables, and almost all the seats were taken. His eyes drifted along the faces, recognizing and nodding to several, until his eyes fell on a face he knew well, too well. Carter Schofield sat next to Judge Ronald Bell and across from U.S. Marshal Strawn Berry.

Jack's face hardened, and his eyes cut through Schofield. Seeing the change, Schofield rose from the table and hurried to Jack, right hand extended.

"Glad you made it back safe. It's good to see you. I'd like to talk—"

Jack ignored the hand. "Get away from me, Carter. This is Mary and Grace's place, so I have no say over it. If I did, I'd throw you out in the street right now. Go sit down and eat, and leave me alone."

Grace, her face flushed from the heat of the kitchen, stepped through the door to the dining room with a radiant smile on her face. The door was close enough for her to hear Jack. The smile fell from her face. She rushed to his side and grasped his arm. "Come, Jack. Join us in back."

The warmth of her hand touched his heart, and he gave her a smile. "It's good to see you." He allowed her to lead him through the entryway into the kitchen. She paused only long enough to push the door closed behind her, then turned to the big ex-lawman.

After throwing her arms around his neck, she stood on her tiptoes. "Kiss me, Jack. Kiss me right now."

He looked around, seeing a strange man at the stove, Mary, and the boys, who were watching with wide eyes and open mouths. "What about the boys?"

She slipped both hands into his hair and pulled his head down. "Don't worry about the boys." She pressed her lips to his.

Jack inhaled the fragrance he had been missing. Her scent of bread mixed with rosewater perfume enveloped him. It invaded his senses, and the loneliness he had traveled with for these past months melted away with the touch and taste of her lips. He crushed her to him, and she came willingly, anxiously.

Moments passed, and when Jack opened his eyes, their lips still touching, he almost laughed. His first sight was the boys. He couldn't figure which was bigger, their eyes or their mouths. He looked back down at Grace. A line of flour drifted along the edge of her jet-black hair, where she had attempted to brush a curl from her eyes. Her face was flushed, eyes bright, and she was more beautiful than when he had first seen her. He smiled down into those big, lovely emerald green eyes. "I've missed you."

"Yes."

"I think we have an audience."

She turned, saw the boys, and broke out in laughter. "Get to work, you two, or I'll give you a kiss."

At the threat, the boys grabbed bowls of food from the table and charged out the door, each grinning and glancing up at Jack as they passed.

Mary, Grace's mother, slipped around the table to Jack and gave him a welcoming kiss on the cheek, then turned to her daughter and, with only a slight tone of reprimand, said, "You don't think that was a little too much?"

Grace, smiling at Jack as she hurried to help the man at the stove, shook her head. "No, Mama, I don't think it was enough."

Mary shook her head and looked up at Jack. "I tried to bring her up right, but she has always been headstrong. Any man who marries her had better hold tight to the reins."

"Mama, don't the boys need some guidance out there?"

Mary smiled sweetly at her daughter, "Yes, dear," and disappeared through the dining-room door. She returned immediately with Judge Bell on her heels. "I'm sorry. I asked him to wait."

The judge stepped past Mary and turned to face Jack's frown. "I apologize for intruding, but I need to speak to Jack."

Grace, both hands on her hips, snapped in return, "Judge

Bell, you know we allow no one back here without an invitation. This is unbelievably rude of you."

The judge inclined his head. "I do apologize, but this is important." He turned to Jack, who was glaring down at him. "We need to talk."

Jack, his voice cold as a winter day in Wyoming, replied, "I'll be in a rocker on the front porch this evening." He stopped and looked at Mary and Grace. "Sorry, I guess I was assuming you might have a room available for me."

Mary gave Jack a smile. "Oh, Jack. Grace made sure we kept your room in the back. The things you left are still there, waiting for you. That room will always be available for you."

"Thanks. That's mighty nice." He looked back down at the judge. "Like I said. If you want to talk, drop by about five. There's another rocker out there. I'm sure the proprietors won't mind."

It was Judge Bell's turn to frown. "This won't wait. I'll see you in my office in one hour."

Jack gave a harsh laugh. "I don't work for you, Judge. You want to talk to me, be here at five, and don't bring Schofield."

The judge's face reddened. "I can send a man for you."

"You better make that *men*, Judge. That means more than two. If I never see the inside of your office again, it'll be too soon."

Judge Bell's face grew redder. He opened his mouth to speak, closed it, took a deep breath, and as calmly as possible said, "I'm asking you, Jack. Please come by my office."

"Judge, this is the last time I'm saying this. I'm not coming to your office. Have a good day." Jack stepped to the dining-room door and held it open.

Through a jaw so clinched it was a wonder he could get the statement out, Judge Bell said, starting for the door, "You best be here at five o'clock." Shoulders back, the judge marched through the open door. When he had passed, Jack released it and took a deep breath, inhaling the smells of the kitchen. "You think you folks could spare a scrap for a worn-out old lawman?"

Grace, who was already piling food on a plate for him, shook her head. "You're not here five minutes, and you've already stolen a kiss and riled the territorial judge. You don't waste time, mister."

The boys had returned to the kitchen and were sitting at their table, shoveling food down. Around a bite of fried chicken, Billy responded, "It didn't look to me like the marshal had to steal it, Ma."

To support his favorite brother, Elijah chimed in, "Yeah."

Everyone laughed, lightening the atmosphere. Grace gave the two boys the eye and then smiled at them. "I don't know what I'm going to do with you two."

Billy spoke up. "I know you'll think of something, Ma."

Mary gave the boys a stern look. "Alright, that's enough of sassing your ma. Eat up. Then you need to pick up some of those dishes before you leave for school. Class will be starting again soon."

The boys settled in to rapidly making their food disappear.

Grace nodded to the man busy washing dishes. "This is Matthew Marcel. He's a chef from New Orleans, and he's headed to Santa Fe. Matthew, this is Mar . . . sorry, Mr. Jack Sage. It's going to take me some time to get used to that."

The man turned and nodded to Jack. "It is a pleasure to meet you, Mr. Sage. I have heard much about you. Welcome home."

"Thanks, Matthew. It's good to be back."

Grace carried Jack's plate to a small table where a steaming cup, partially filled with coffee, awaited him, along with sugar and a small pitcher of thick cream. "Come over here and sit down, Jack. Give your things to the boys, and they'll put them in your room. You need to eat."

Jack handed his rifle to Billy and his saddlebags to Elijah. "Thanks, boys. You know to be careful."

They both nodded and spoke in unison, "Yes, sir," and walked sedately out of the kitchen and down the hallway.

Grace sat down with him while he added sugar and cream to

his coffee. "Oh, Jack. We heard what happened. It made it to our paper, which means it was printed all over the country. That man saved your life?"

Jack took a long sip of his coffee. It was just right. He set his cup down and placed a big paw over her strong but delicate-looking hand. "Yeah, Grace. If he hadn't of been there, we wouldn't be talking right now." He gave a long sigh. "And then I killed him, in a useless gunfight that should never have happened. I've had too many of those." He gazed into her green eyes. "We've got enough money to go anywhere, with the boys and Mary. Money will never be a worry. It's time I stop saving people and worry about my own life, and yours."

Tears filled her eyes. Her free hand dropped over his, and she squeezed. "Jack, I don't care where we go or what we do. I just want to be with you. I want you to put this killing behind you and live happily for the rest of your life."

The big ex-lawman smiled. "Well, this sounds like what one of those traveling actors might call a cue." Jack slid his chair back, enjoying the surprised look on Grace's face. Her red lips pressed together in surprise, and the green of her eyes appeared to deepen. He removed his hat and, sensing the importance of the moment, extended it by combing his thick brown hair back with his fingers. Slowly he reached into a bulging vest pocket and removed a small box before dropping to his right knee.

Grace's lips had parted in anticipation. The boys, running back from his room, slid to a stop, sensing this was something important that would affect their future as much as it would their mother's. Mary walked back in, carrying a stack of dirty plates. She halted, immediately recognizing what was happening. Her eyes filled with tears, and a soft smile stretched her lips.

Jack dropped to a knee and opened the box. "I found this in St. Louis. It's different. It reminded me of your eyes. I hope you like it." It was a gold ring with a single stone, a large green emerald floating alone in a sea of gold.

"Grace Kathryn Blakely, I've searched a long time to find the right woman. You are the kindest, most loving person I've ever met, and I don't want to lose you. Would you put an old lawman out of his misery? Will you marry me?" The ring slipped perfectly on her finger. "Well, I'll be darned. It fits."

Tears flowed softly down her cheeks, and she took his face in her hands. "I have been so hoping you would ask, Jack. You are the best man in the world. Yes, definitely yes."

Jack kissed her lightly and pulled his head back. "You've made a happy man of me, Grace. Now can I get up? My knee is killing me."

Laughing, she slapped him on the shoulder to the applause of Mary and Matthew. "For goodness' sake, Jack, get up. You're no spring chicken." The boys joined in half-heartedly, not yet understanding what this meant for them. Their applause drew her attention. "Oh, my goodness. You boys are late. Miss Hawkins will be upset. Tell her to talk to me, and I'll explain. Now give me a hug, and get out of here."

Each of the boys ran to her, then in turn also gave Jack and Mary a quick hug. Then they dashed from the kitchen. Dodging the speeding boys, Buck stepped through the dining-room door.

7

Buck's gaze swept the kitchen. Matthew was turning back to the dishes. Mary and Grace wore wide smiles while both dabbed at their eyes, and something most people seldom saw, Jack Sage with his guard down, was pulling his attention from Grace. "Sorry to bust in. Did I interrupt something?"

Mary regained her composure before Grace. "Well, Buck . . ." She looked at Jack, who shrugged, and Grace, still smiling, gave a tiny nod with her head, and Mary continued, "It looks like you'll be the first to know. Jack just asked Grace for her hand."

In confusion, Buck frowned, failing to comprehend. "Her hand?"

Jack rolled his eyes. "You knucklehead, I asked her to marry me."

A grin spread across Buck's face. He shoved his hat to the back of his head and put his hands on his hips. "Well, knock me over with a Comanche feather." Then he yanked his hat from atop his head, whipped his arm across his waist, and gave Grace an exaggerated bow. "Congratulations, ma'am. I've got to say, you look mighty pleased and mighty pretty. Though I don't know how you'll be able to control this big galoot and keep him from gallivanting all over the country."

Jack glared at Buck. "Did you have something constructive to say?"

Grace tempered Jack's question with a smile. "Thank you, Buck. I'm sure Jack will do whatever he feels is necessary."

"Yes, ma'am, thanks." He grew serious. "I do need to talk to Jack."

Still frowning, Jack pointed to the front door. "Let's step outside." His frown turned to a smile when he looked at Grace. "I'll be back in a few minutes."

She returned the smile and moved to Matthew's side, picking up a dish towel and a plate. "Take your time. I'll be right here." She stretched out her right hand and gazed at the new ring that rode so perfectly on her finger.

Buck pushed through the dining-room door, Jack on his heels. They stepped outside into the cool February afternoon. The sun shone down on them through clear skies. A light breeze from the south rustled the pine needles, drifting the scent of pines across Ma's Bed and Eats.

Jack moved to the line of rockers and carefully lowered himself into the largest. He leaned back, tilted his hat forward, leaving a small space for his eyes, and began to rock. "You sitting or standing?"

Buck dropped into a rocker alongside. "I needed to talk to you."

Jack's rocker squeaked with each rock.

"Needs a little beeswax," Buck said, one side of his mouth lifting in a mischievous grin. "You'll be getting a lot of them honey-dos before long."

Jack shot Buck a sharp glance from beneath the brim of his hat. "You may think you're fast enough to get out of my reach, but you're gonna be in for a real surprise. Now, what's on your mind?"

"Judge Bell needs to see you."

"I've already had that discussion with him. He'll be by later, and we'll have a talk."

Buck leaned closer. "Jack, he doesn't have the time. He's got over thirty deputy marshals, most bringing in lawbreakers every day. He runs his court as long as twelve hours a day and sometimes longer." Buck's head shook back and forth. "You know what the Indian Territory is like. Outlaws outnumber the honest folks. They're packed into the court's prison. The marshals are bringing them in faster than the judge can try them. His time is used up every day."

Jack was silent, his rocker continuing to squeak. At last he spoke. "You mentioned Barrett Clagg when I rode in. Are there any more details about his escape?"

Buck took off his hat, releasing his curly brown hair and allowing it to drop around his ears. The deputy placed his hat on his lap. "There ain't much more, Jack. Judge Bell had sentenced Clagg to hang for killing Franklin. It was supposed to take place when Clagg was well enough to be hanged, if that makes any sense at all. In my opinion, they should've tried him and let him stretch a rope that day. Several weeks later, before the scheduled hanging, Clagg up and kills one of the guards and just walks out, free and clear, in the guard's uniform. The other guards followed his tracks to a spot in the trees where someone waited with horses. They tried to follow him, but he got across the river and disappeared. That's only been a week or so ago, but there's been no report of him anywhere."

Jack continued to rock. "He'll have a hard time shooting anyone with that right hand."

"You're not joking. The doc had to cut off his three middle fingers and the first joint of his thumb. He might as well not have any hand at all."

"I was hoping he might see the light and go straight."

"Pshaw, Jack. He's a Clagg. All of them fellers were crookeder than snakes. He'll never change."

Buck tapped the arm of Jack's rocker for emphasis. "I'll tell you something else. He'll learn how to shoot with his left hand. When he does, he'll be coming after you. It may not be soon, but it'll surely happen. I promise you."

Jack chuckled. "He won't be the first." But then he thought of Grace, Mary, and the boys and felt a cloud of concern drift over him. *I never had anyone to think about other than myself. Now, I have a family. They need to be protected.*

Buck stood. "I'm just saying, you best stay on the lookout."

Jack stopped rocking, pushed his hat up, and looked at his friend. "Thanks, Buck. I'm obliged. Believe me, I will."

"Good. You coming to see the judge?"

"Nope. Like I told him, I'll be out here in a rocker at five o'clock. I'll be glad to talk to him then, *alone*."

"I don't catch your drift, Jack."

"The judge will." He stood. "Now you get on about your business, or Berry'll be docking your pay."

Buck snorted. "Ain't that the truth. See you around." Buck turned and headed across the busy street, for the marshal's office.

Jack gave the street a thorough once-over. Assessing the buildings and street free of danger, Jack thought, *I've got to settle up with Pauly, but first I need to let Grace know. We also need to talk about what comes after the marriage. I'd like to head back to Texas, but she may be fed up with the frontier.* He stepped to the door.

Moving into the parlor, Jack found Grace sitting alone. She turned as he stepped inside, and began to rise. He smiled and shook his head. "Keep your seat. We need to talk."

She is such a vision, he thought. Though her lovely black hair had been pulled back in a severe bun, the hairdo could do nothing to subtract from her beauty. It framed her fair skin, which was kissed by the sun, giving it a rich golden glow. It framed her striking, large, emerald-green eyes. Above a strong chin, those wide red lips were partly open. Those eyes followed his movement into the room.

"Grace, you are a beautiful woman."

Her cheeks glowed pink from his comment. "Jack, I think you might be slightly prejudiced."

He laughed. "If I am, then so is every man in Fort Smith. Your marrying me will break a lot of hearts."

Her laughter filled the room. She was sitting in one of the wingback chairs, and Jack sat on the loveseat facing her. She reached across and slapped him on a knee. "You are so fibbing. You're going to make me get out the lye soap."

He grinned at her. "That sounds like fun."

"Jack." She slapped his knee again.

He grew serious. "I wanted to talk to you. Do you have any idea what you would like to do after we're married?"

She leaned back in the deep cushions of the wingback. "After we're married, doesn't that sound delicious?"

His grin widened. "It sounds mighty good to me, too. Maybe we ought to just go down to the courthouse and get it done."

She leaned forward in the chair, a touch of seriousness removing the smile. "I would love to, right now, but Mama is set on us getting married in the church by a minister with all our friends around us. Would you mind?"

Jack shook his head. "I don't mind at all." He paused before continuing, "As long as it happens pretty soon."

She clapped her hands. "Oh, yes, me too. I can hardly wait."

"Can hardly wait for what, dear?" Mary walked in and sat next to Jack on the loveseat.

Grace blushed and winked at Jack. "To get married, Mama. Jack and I were talking about walking down to the courthouse and having Judge Bell perform the ceremony today."

Mary frowned. "You'll do no such thing. You two can wait a while longer. It takes time to do this type of thing correctly."

Jack, who towered over Grace's diminutive mother, frowned. "How much time?"

"At least a month."

It was Grace who spoke up. "A month. Good gracious, Mama, what kind of soiree are you planning?"

Mary's mouth tightened. "I am not planning a soiree, Grace. I just want you to have a wedding that will be memorable."

"Ma'am," Jack interrupted, having a vague feeling he should instead make himself scarce, "isn't any marriage memorable to the folks getting married?"

Mary, sitting straight and as tall as possible, turned to face Jack. He felt like a battery of cannons were being repositioned to fire on him. "It is important for a woman to be surrounded by her friends and family on such a momentous occasion."

Jack stood. He nodded to his future wife and his future mother-in-law. "I've got to admit, this is something I know nothing about. If you two can work it out and just let me know when and where I need to be, I'd appreciate it."

Grace smiled. "Must you leave?"

"Reckon I should. I owe Pauly for the horses, and I need to stop by the bank. Also, the judge is supposed to be by to talk at five."

Grace held her smile. "It sounds like you are very busy, Jack."

"Seems so." He stepped to the door. "Ladies." Once through, he pulled the door closed and let out a long sigh of relief, thinking, *Who ever thought this wedding was such a big event? Guess I won't be bringing it up again.*

Jack surveyed the streets and buildings. Several marshals lounged along the street, but he knew they weren't just taking in the sights. They were looking for trouble. Clagg's escape had created more concern than the law and courts were releasing. With the surroundings clear, Jack stepped into the street and headed for his first stop, the bank. He needed to withdraw a little more money. The money he had received from his part ownership in the gold mine in New Mexico and the Texas ranch had come in handy.

A team pulling a freight wagon swerved toward him as they

were passing. He jumped back just in time to prevent the mules from grinding him into the already pulverized dirt. The front wheel was inches from his face as it rolled past. The teamster yelled at the mules and jerked the reins. Jack figured his size kept him from getting a thorough cussing from the man, but he received an angry stare. The team passed in an instant, and Jack continued across the street. He chuckled to himself while thinking, *Wouldn't that be great, survive all the gunfights and ambushes to be crushed to death by a freight wagon after I've hung up my badge?*

He was still chuckling when he shoved the bank's door open. Casey Carter stood behind the protecting bars, his smiling face there to greet him. "Hi, Casey. I figured you would be on your way west and into your next adventure by the time I returned."

The young bank teller's smile spread to a wide grin. "When I gave Mr. Gleason my notice, he offered me a raise. He made it so good, I thought I'd stay a little longer until I had a really good stake. That way, I can buy a fine horse and first-rate equipment."

"Just be careful. Before you know it, you'll be meeting a nice girl who lives in Fort Smith, and this will be as far west as you get."

Casey smiled sheepishly. "I've already met a girl."

"Well, that's a good thing. I'd like to meet her. Maybe you could introduce us sometime."

"Yes, sir, I'd like that. She's Mr. Gleason's daughter."

"Very nice. I hope you two are happy. Now, I need to withdraw two hundred dollars. Split it up like you did before."

Before Casey could answer, a call came from the back office. "Marshal Sage, it's good to see you. Perhaps you could step back here for a few minutes while Casey gets your money ready?"

"I'll be right back, Marley." Jack saw the banker wince at the use of his first name. He smiled to himself, stepped to the pony wall, which ran past the teller's cage, swung the door open, and strode back to Marley Gleason's office.

The banker stood at his doorway, hand extended. "Marshal Sage, welcome back. Please step inside for a moment."

Jack took the extended hand. "It's Jack, Marley. I'm no longer a marshal. Just a man of leisure for now."

"Oh, well, my, my. Of course, it was of your own doing. I can see where a man would grow tired of traipsing around the countryside looking for bandits and killers, only to be paid a pittance." The banker's eyes brightened. "And, of course, your newfound wealth. We mustn't forget that."

Jack said nothing.

The banker motioned to one of two straight-backed chairs in front of his desk. "Please, take a seat." After closing the door, he moved to his large, cushioned leather chair behind his desk and lowered his bulk onto the padded leather. He leaned forward, resting his arms on his massive oak table. "I needed to tell you, Jack, only three days after you left, you received another deposit from New Mexico. This one was not as big, but still substantial. It was in the amount of seventy-five thousand dollars. Your mine must be doing quite well."

Surprised, Jack nodded. "I'd say so, and to think I made that find while attempting to evade killers." He gave Gleason an innocent grin. "Sometimes the law does pay off."

Gleason cleared his throat. "Well, yes, I get your meaning, but concerning your new funds, what would you like us to do with it? There are some fine investment opportunities here in Fort Smith. I'd be more than happy to advise you on them, for a small commission, of course."

Jack eyed the banker. "Marley, can you tell me how much is in my account?"

Gleason smiled. "It just so happens I have the total in front of me. It is one hundred ninety-three thousand and nine hundred dollars. That's minus the thousand you took out before your trip, the other two-hundred-dollar withdrawal, and the fifty thousand you transferred to Ma's Bed and Eats account. It is quite a substantial amount, if I do say so. You are a very wealthy man, Mr. Sage. Of course, this total will be minus whatever it is you take today."

Jack stood. "Thanks, Marley. I'll let you know if I need any further help. Have a good day."

Surprised, Gleason jumped to his feet and began to extend his hand, but Jack was already out the door, calling, "Hey, Casey, when are you going to have lunch with me?"

Casey Carter grinned. "Anytime, Marshal Sage. I go to lunch at noon. I only have thirty minutes, so it'll have to be fast."

"Are you available tomorrow?"

"Yes, sir."

Jack turned and yelled back at Gleason, "Hey, Marley, you don't mind if I steal your teller tomorrow for an extended lunch, do you?"

Gleason stepped from his office. "He does have work to do around here, Jack, but no, I guess that would be fine."

Jack grinned at the fat man. "Good." He turned back to Casey. "You have some money for me?"

Casey, his grin so large it looked like it would break his face, stacked the gold and silver coins. He looked up at Jack when he said, "One hundred dollars."

Jack nodded his agreement. Casey collected and placed the coins into a leather pouch and handed it to Jack. Next, he counted out the remaining hundred in bills, and Jack swept them up, folding them and stuffing the paper money into a vest pocket. "Thanks, Casey. I'll meet you at Ma's Bed and Eats at noon tomorrow. Bring an appetite."

Jack could see the excitement playing across Casey's face. "I'll be there. Thanks, Mr. Sage."

"Call me Jack, boy. I'll see you then." Through Casey's teller cage, Jack could see Gleason sitting in his office, listening to every word. A frown stamped on his face. When he saw Jack watching, his frown changed to a smile, and he nodded. Jack gave him a wave and was out the front door.

Remembering his encounter with Barrett Clagg a couple of months ago at the bank, he shook his head and thought, *It's hard to believe Clagg broke out. I know he'll come after me. The man looked completely serious when he threatened to kill me. I hope he hurries it up so I can take care of him before I have Grace and the boys around me.*

He continued to Pauly's stable, paid him for two weeks, greeted his animals, and, after checking the time, headed back to the boardinghouse. When he stepped onto the boardwalk, Jack removed his pocket watch and checked the time. His thumb drifted over the carved emerald embedded in the watch's front. *I've found someone, Yasmina,* Jack thought. *I hope you don't mind.* He felt a spirit of peace settle over him. It was so real he rubbed his chest, almost expecting to feel her soft hand. Nothing. He took an overly deep breath, released it in a long sigh, and gazed down the boardwalk.

Jack could see Judge Bell striding toward him, confidence in his step. He had two companions with him. The first strode with the same confidence as the judge. He was Marshal Strawn Berry, but the second didn't appear quite so confident. Since the first time he had met him, Jack had never seen Carter Schofield so beside himself. This drastic change piqued his curiosity but not enough to engage him in conversation.

8

Jack felt his scalp begin to tingle. *It's best if I have nothing to do with Carter,* Jack thought. *Otherwise, I'm liable to tear him apart or fill him so full of holes he'll make a good martin house.*

The men stopped, and the judge nodded. "Jack, I'm here."

Jack glared at Carter. "What's he doing here?"

Carter started to respond, and Judge Bell held up a hand. "He almost insisted he be allowed to come along for this meeting. He gave me several valid reasons, so I let him."

Jack turned to go inside. "Good, Judge. You two can talk about whatever interests you. I won't be involved."

Judge Bell snapped, "Jack, quit acting like a child."

Jack was reaching for the door when Judge Bell made his comment. He spun around. He couldn't believe his ears. This judge was calling him a child. Judge Bell was not a small man, but Jack towered over him.

He glared down at the man until Marshal Berry stepped up. "Jack."

Jack slowly turned his head to meet Berry's steady eyes, held them for a moment, and started for the door.

"Jack," the judge called.

He didn't stop. Usually cool in conflict, this judge could always light his fire. He was done with these people.

Jack had played Reno's draw constantly in his mind, and the causation, Carter's hand driving under his coat. The answer had come to him, and with it, the realization Carter Schofield could no longer be trusted. Not the man or anything he represented as being from the president. He reached for the handle.

"Jack, wait. I'm sorry. My last comment was uncalled for."

Jack stopped. *Am I hearing correctly?* he thought. *Is the judge apologizing?* He released the handle and turned around.

"Jack, we really need to talk."

"Judge, this is the last time I'll say this. I'll talk to you but without Carter Schofield. I know him to be untrustworthy, and I don't know how much further it goes."

The judge studied Carter, then turned back to Jack. "If we meet alone, will you come to my office? I believe the things we need to discuss should be in confidence."

"Alright, Judge, but understand, I am through carrying a badge, so if that's what you have planned, this is a waste of time."

The judge stepped forward and laid his hand on Jack's thick shoulder. "Talk to me, Jack. That's all I ask."

Judge Bell and Jack started for the courthouse. Marshal Berry fell in behind with Schofield alongside him. At the sound of the boots, Jack halted and whipped around, pointing at Schofield. "You! Hold it right there. I know what you did. If I had figured it out in Independence, I would've thrown you in jail. Stay away from me."

Carter Schofield looked like he had been slapped. He appeared to shrink in stature. He handed a sealed envelope to Judge Bell and, without a word of argument, walked away.

Nesbit occupied the desk outside the judge's office when the trio walked in. Seeing Jack, he stood and opened his mouth to offer a greeting, but at Marshal Berry's head shake, said nothing. The three men entered the judge's office.

After entering, Judge Bell turned to Berry. "Strawn, would you wait outside?"

The marshal hesitated, eyed Jack for a moment, then stepped out of the office, pulling the door shut. Judge Bell pointed to the divan in his office. "Sit, Jack. Coffee?"

Jack shook his head, immediately suspicious. "No coffee, Judge." Being pleasant was not usually on the judge's agenda.

The judge moved to the far end of the couch, sat, and, raising his voice, called through the closed door, "Nesbit."

The door opened immediately. Deputy Marshal Nesbit asked, "Yes, Judge."

"Would you get me a coffee, please?"

The deputy glanced at Jack, who shook his head.

He closed the door.

"Jack, I have something for you from the president."

"You can keep it, Judge. I'm done. I'm not complaining, but I've spent most of my life taking care of other people. The years are stacking up, and before I create any additional enemies, I'm going to have a life of my own."

Jack was a smart man. He knew the judge was used to getting his way, usually with a club and not honey. The man was having a hard time curbing his anger.

"Jack, I don't know what happened in Missouri, and I don't care. It's obvious Carter did something, but it's none of my business. It took place outside of my jurisdiction. I'm asking you, man to man, to read this letter. It is from your president, your friend. Read it, and my job's done. We can part ways, friends."

Jack caught the veiled threat. He ignored it and thought, *Bell's right. The president is my friend, although I trust nothing delivered by Schofield, but reading the letter does no harm.* Jack held out a hand. "I'll read it."

Instant relief covered the judge's face. "Thank you, Jack." He handed him the letter. "I'll step out."

Jack shook his head. "Not necessary." He felt the light weight of the contents of the letter. "This won't take long."

"I need a cup of coffee, and Nesbit will be coming back up the stairs shortly. Anyway, if you'll notice on the letter, it states it is to be read in private."

For the first time, Jack looked at the envelope. On the front, in large letters, was written, *Open in Private, by order of the President*, signed, *Ulysses S. Grant*.

Jack looked up at the judge, whose hand was already on the door. "Alright, thanks, Judge."

Judge Bell stepped from the room, pulling the door closed behind him.

Jack slipped his Barlow from his pocket, slid the blade under the edge of the envelope, and sliced through the paper. Staring at the edge of the folded contents inside the envelope, Jack felt a momentary sense of dread, then put it aside. It mattered little what the president wanted. He was done marshaling.

He shoved a thumb and forefinger inside the envelope, latched onto the letter, and yanked it out. Jack read through the letter. The first few sentences were words of gratitude relayed from Senator Harris for bringing a killer to justice. Jack's jaws clenched. He continued reading. From the president's tone, it was clear Schofield had reported everything, but in a way that exonerated him and continued the farce that Reno was a killer and Sean Harris Jr. an innocent victim. By the time he finished reading, Jack was livid. He rose and stepped to the door.

Deputy Nesbit was sipping a cup of coffee at his desk. He began to rise, and Jack waved him down. "Nesbit, do you have any paper and an official envelope? I need to answer the president."

"I sure do, Jack." He pulled open a lower side drawer and, from a file, pulled several sheets of paper. From an adjacent folder, he removed an envelope. "Here you go, Jack. The judge has a pen on his desk. I'm sure he won't mind you using it. Judge Bell will be a while. He had a case that will take a bit, but I was asked to tell you he'd like to talk to you before you leave."

Jack took the paper and envelope. He knew how the judge asked, more like a command. "Thanks. It's going to take me a while. I'm writing a report for the president. I'll be out as soon as I've finished."

"No problem, Jack. The judge left orders you were not to be disturbed."

Jack stepped back into the office, moved around the desk, and took a seat in the judge's chair. He pulled the pen to him, positioned the paper, and began to write. *It's time,* he thought, *for the president to find out what actually happened.*

In the letter, Jack clarified the background information, pointing out that though he was a gambler, Reno Flint was a good and honest man. He also explained his information of what happened in the sheriff's office could be backed up by the sheriff and his deputies. As far as the shooting of Sean Harris Jr., the sheriff and witnesses would also back up Reno Flint's account. At last, his writing took him to the final page, where he explained about the shooting and the conclusion he had come to concerning Schofield's actions. He also explained why he was done with being a lawman, and, the important point, he would not be persuaded to put on a badge again. Jack finished and signed the letter.

After allowing the three pages to dry, he folded them, slid the missive into the envelope, sealed it, and wrote on both sides of the envelope, *President's Eyes Only!* Jack positioned the ink and well in its previous location and returned the leather chair to its regular position. He strode to the divan and was about to sit when the door opened. It was the judge.

"You were leaving?"

Jack shook his head. "No, sir." He held the document out to the judge, who took it and examined the inscription on the front.

"I'll give this to Carter. After you two meet, he'll be going back to Washington."

"First," Jack said, "there will be no meeting. Second, this dispatch needs to be sent to Washington in a pouch not accessible to Carter Schofield."

The judge closed his door, tapping the envelope against his opposite hand while he stepped around to his desk. He sat and waited for Jack to drop into a wingback nearer the desk. "This is highly unusual, Jack." The judge opened a shallow drawer in his desk and removed another dispatch from the president. "In this, he mentions another task he has asked you to do, and he also says Carter will communicate the information to you."

Jack nodded. "He also mentioned it in the letter I received. I have taken care of that mission by explaining to the president I resign from law enforcement. I was in hopes he would have gotten the message when I shoved my badge into Carter's hand in Independence. Obviously he didn't. I set a bad precedent by taking the badge back the last time. I should have stuck to my guns then." Jack stared out the window, noticing for the first time it was growing dark, then continued, "But since I didn't, I accepted the mission and killed a good man. That won't be happening again." Jack stood.

"Thank you for persuading me to talk. I needed to write that letter. It has some highly sensitive information in it. I need your word you will ensure it goes back to the president by a different courier than Schofield."

"Jack, is that necessary?"

"Judge, I wouldn't be asking if it wasn't necessary. Now I need your word."

"I find this rather insulting."

Jack's hand flashed across the desk, and he yanked the dispatch from the judge. "Don't worry about it, Judge Bell. I'll take it to the army post. I'm sure I'll be able to get it in a secure pouch there." He turned to leave.

The judge leaped to his feet. "Just a minute, Sage."

Jack had never been a patient man, especially when it came to politics. He could feel his patience running out. "Yes, Bell?"

"You listen to me, young man." Bell's voice rose. "I am the territorial judge in these parts, appointed by the president of the United States. You will treat me with the proper respect. You don't jerk anything out of my hands. Do you understand me?"

There was a knock on the door. "Come in!" The request was loud enough to have been heard in the courtroom.

Deputy Nesbit slowly opened the door just wide enough to stick his head in. "Everything alright, Judge?"

"Yes. Why wouldn't it be?"

"Thank you, sir." The deputy's head disappeared, and the door closed.

"I asked you a question, Jack."

"I know who you are, Judge. The problem is, I don't know what you are. Are you a judge or a politician? You see my problem?" Jack waved the envelope. "This has to get to the president intact. He needs to know what is going on in the field to make proper decisions. If it falls into the wrong hands, he won't get this information."

The judge's anger faded as his curiosity grew. "Is this something I should know?"

Jack shook his head. "Not before the president."

Bell shook his head. "I don't like this, keeping information from the president's representative."

Jack was silent.

"Alright, Jack, if you'll trust me, I will see this goes into a separate, secure pouch. This pouch will only be opened by the president's people, and they will see he gets your letter. It will not be given to Carter, though this may be the end of my career."

Jack handed the judge the envelope, but as the judge tried to take it, Jack held onto it. "Your word?"

Bell sighed. "I give you my word. Carter Schofield will not get this document."

Jack released it to the judge's hand. "Thanks, Judge."

"One more thing, Jack. You are serious. You are no longer a marshal and will not carry out marshal's duties?"

"That's correct."

"Then I'll have to take you off the payroll."

Jack grinned. "I think I can handle that, Judge."

Judge Bell, apparently remembering about Jack's gold mine, allowed a tiny grin to raise one corner of his mouth. "Yes, I suppose you can. What are your plans now?"

"At the moment, they're a little up in the air, but as soon as they firm up, I'll let you know."

The judge's eyebrows rose, and he gave an inquisitive nod. "Hmmm, a riddle. I am curious. Let me know when you can." He extended his hand. "Good luck to you, Jack. We haven't always agreed, but I never doubted your honesty or where you stood."

Jack took it. "Thanks, Judge. It's been a pleasure." He opened the door, closing it after stepping out, and passing Deputy Nesbit's desk. He raised a hand in salute and headed down the stairs. *I'm late for supper,* Jack thought, *and I've built up a raging appetite.*

The moment Jack stepped out the door of the courthouse, a rifle blasted in the night, and a bullet tugged at his left shoulder. Jack dove to the left. When his hands hit the banister, his long legs propelled him up and over. From the stairway landing of the courthouse, he knew it was at least ten feet to the ground. He was leaping into a black hole. Jack sailed up and over the railing, plunging to the surface below.

It seemed like forever before he hit, and his two hundred and five pounds drove him to the ground. His right shoulder plowed into the earth as he rolled, and when he came up, a Smith & Wesson revolver, with hammer eared back, was gripped in his right hand. There were shrubs encircling the courthouse. Jack hugged them to break his outline and froze, waiting.

No other shots were fired. Doors were opening, and light was flooding the street. *Which is good,* he thought. *The light might catch the shooter as he's trying to escape.* Jack had no more than had the thought when he spotted a vague shadow, rifle in hand, dash from one alley to another and disappear.

Jack hadn't even tried to take a shot. The target was too far, running at night. Furthermore, it could've been some citizen trying to save himself from being shot. The courthouse door burst open, and Nesbit charged out, gun in hand. He stopped on the landing, looking around into the darkness.

"You out there, Jack?"

Jack stood, dropping his revolver back into its holster. "Yep, still here."

"You hurt?"

"Nothing more than a sore shoulder from jumping over the banister in the dark. That was a smart move."

Nesbit chuckled. "Yeah, that's a long way down, and the ground is mighty hard. You're not hit?"

"No," Jack said, staying in the darkness. "Whoever took the shot must've known I was in the courthouse, and was waiting for me to be backlighted when I came out."

Marshal Berry ran up. "What's going on?" he asked Nesbit about the time the judge and several of the late workers came out of the courthouse.

"Someone took a shot at Jack." He nodded toward Jack, who was standing in the darkness, his outline barely visible.

Berry squinted toward Jack. "You alright?"

"Fit as a fiddle. He missed. I might need a sleeve repaired, but that's as close as he got."

Berry examined the street in both directions. People who had charged out at the shot were now going back into their homes.

Doors were closing, and light was disappearing along the street. "Whoever it was knew you were in the courthouse."

Nesbit nodded. "That's what Jack was saying."

Several other folks had gathered around the courthouse steps, listening. One was Carter Schofield. He squinted toward Jack. "You alright?"

Jack stepped to Berry's side. "I'm hungry. I think I'll see if I can get Grace to whip up a few crumbs."

His statement elicited a grin from Berry. "From what I've heard, that shouldn't be too difficult."

Jack stared at the marshal, shrugged, and let it pass. "Hopefully. See you later."

Berry turned serious. "Keep your eyes open. I haven't seen Clagg around, but he did escape. It could be him, although I don't think so. He's carrying a mighty big grudge. I think he'd much rather face you."

Jack nodded. "I agree." He turned and headed toward the boardinghouse. Not liking the thoughts that were playing in his mind. *Would he actually try to ambush me?* Jack chewed on his suspicions until he reached the boardinghouse, then put them aside and opened the door, stepping into the parlor.

He was met with a rush. Grace threw her arms around him and pulled him close. "I'm so glad you're safe. You could've been killed."

He put his arms around her slim waist and pulled her to him, kissing the top of her head. "If I'm gonna get this kind of welcome every time some yahoo takes a shot at me, I may start setting them up."

Grace stepped back and slapped him on his shoulder. "Careful, mister! You could get in big trouble."

The blow carried a pretty good wallop that sent pain into his neck. He moved his shoulder around, checking. The fall could have pulled something.

Concerned, Grace reached for his shoulder. "Did I hurt you?"

Several guests sat in the parlor, enjoying a cigar after supper. A man who looked like a gunfighter or a prosperous rancher spoke up. "Ma'am, I could be wrong, but I'd reckon you'd have to hit that feller with a crosstie to hurt him."

Grace spun around, a touch of anger on her face, lips pursed. "Mr. Livingston, he was just shot at. How about a little more respect?"

The man smiled at her irritation. "Sorry, ma'am. I imagine Mr. Sage there probably figures your welcome was worth that bullet."

Jack laughed at the response. "I'm forced to say you are right as rain." He turned Grace around. "I'm fine except for being so hungry I could eat the south end of a northbound mule."

This time, she slapped him on the other shoulder. "Jack! Don't be so crude in front of our guests. Now come into the kitchen and let me see if I can find a few leftovers, and you can tell me all about what happened."

9

Jack was up early and helped the boys with their chores. They were excited and begged him to tell them what had happened during the shooting last night. He filled them in, and then they were full of questions about who it could have been. Both boys came up with the wildest ideas. Helping them had left him little time to discuss his thoughts about their future with Grace. On the one hand, Jack wasn't in a rush, but on the other . . .

At breakfast, all the talk was about Jack's shooting the previous night. Though he was prodded with questions, Jack had no idea who it could have been.

Livingston, who was a rancher, a gunfighter, or both, chimed in, "If nobody knows who it could've been, then odds are he'll try again."

The remark brought silence to the table. Mary had been carrying a full bowl of biscuits to the crowded table. "I swear, you men gossip worse than a gaggle of women." Her comment brought laughter and denials, but changed the subject, and she winked at Jack.

When Jack finished, he tried to help, but the women drove

him out, so he walked the boys to school. Mrs. Hawkins gave him a pleasant greeting, but hurried Billy and Elijah into the school building and pulled the door closed. He stood among the trees, hearing and feeling the echoes of the playing children, who were all secure inside the schoolhouse. A few seconds passed, and the big ex-marshal sighed and headed for Pauly's stable. Throughout his life, Jack had always had something to do. As a seaman, legionnaire, soldier, Texas Ranger, or marshal, he had always been busy. He had a purpose. Having nothing to do was going to drive him crazy. *I'll give the animals a good rubdown,* he thought. *If I do all four of them, that should get me almost to dinner.*

Jack walked into the stable and saw Pauly speaking to the Livingston who had been staying at Ma's Bed and Eats. He nodded to the two of them, noticing that Pauly's head followed him as he walked by. Stonewall was the first to spot Jack, and his big head tracked his approach. He slapped the mule on its rump and turned to Pauly. "You have any cookies?"

Pauly interrupted his conversation by holding up a finger to Livingston. "You can find 'em in the tack room. I can't leave them out here, or folks will eat 'em."

"Mind if I get five?"

Pauly shook his head. "Go ahead. Get as many as you want."

Jack found the cookie sack hanging in the tack room and stuffed two in his pockets, keeping the remaining three in his hands. Stonewall was his first stop. Then he made his way to each, enjoying the way they crunched the cookies. Finished, he pulled out the remaining one and began to add to the crunch noise. With his last bite, Pauly called, "Hey, Jack, can you step over here?"

Jack took another bite and strolled to where the two men were standing. He nodded. "Mr. Livingston, how are you doing today?"

"It's Art, Jack, if I can call you that, and not too well. Seems Pauly sold me some stock and was supposed to have another drover here to help me get them back to Little Rock. The man's gone."

Pauly rolled his eyes at Jack. "It's Snuffy."

Jack shook his head. "Say no more. Do you know where he is?"

"I have no idea. He was supposed to be here right now, ready to go. But Jack, I was thinking. I know you've got a little time on your hands. Would you be interested in giving Art a hand, driving some stock back to his spread? It's back Little Rock way, 'bout halfway."

Jack thought for a minute. "I don't know, Pauly. Grace is supposed to be coming through with plans. I'm kind of in a holding pen right now."

"I'm really in a bind, Jack. I promised Art, and he needs to get back home. If pay is a problem, rest assured you'll be paid."

"Shoot no, Pauly. Don't worry about the pay. I'll be glad to do it. What are we driving and how many?"

Art spoke up. "Horses. Twenty-five. I need to get them moving. They're in a corral south of town."

"I've got to tell you, I'm not the best roper in the world."

Art shook his head. "It doesn't matter. I need a body to help me get these animals home. You'll be just fine. Any roping you can't handle, I'll do it."

Jack nodded. "Then I'm your man. I've got to tell Grace and grab my gear. Pauly, would you saddle Pepper for me? He needs some work."

Pauly started for the tack room. "Glad to do it, Jack. Thanks for helping me out. You've saved my reputation."

Jack raised a hand in acknowledgment and headed for the boardinghouse. He figured it wouldn't be a big deal for Grace. Guests, meals, and the boys kept her busy all day. This way, he'd be out of everyone's way for a few days. It would give her time to decide what she and Mary wanted to do about the wedding. He nodded, stepping onto the boardwalk and opening the door.

Removing his hat to keep from knocking it to the floor on the door's overhead, he bent and entered the parlor. Speaking to himself as he often did in the saddle, he said, "This'll be good for everyone."

"What will be good, Jack?"

Surprised, he turned toward the pleasant voice. Grace sat in the green wingback chair in the corner of the parlor most distant from the door. She had a book in her lap and a welcoming smile on her face.

Jack strode to her side, bent, and gave her a long enjoyable kiss, which she returned with enthusiasm. He lifted his head and smiled into those bright eyes. "I love you, Grace."

Her chest rose, and tears filled her eyes. "Oh, Jack. Do you know that's the first time you've told me you love me? I love you, too, so much." She stood and moved to the love seat, holding her hand out to him. "Come, sit with me for a few minutes. The boys are in school, and Mama went to the store. I don't think any of our guests are in right now. Give me another kiss."

As tempted as he was, Jack shook his head. "Sorry, honey. I've got to pack and get going. Pauly asked me to help Art Livingston drive the horses he just bought from him back to his ranch."

Grace stiffened. "You are leaving?"

"Just for a few days. I'll be back in no time." He grinned at her. "As busy as you are, you won't even know I'm gone."

Jack watched the smile disappear from Grace's face. "Jack, aren't we supposed to be planning a wedding?"

For a moment, Jack was at a loss for words. He had been all but driven from their wedding discussion. This didn't make sense. "Honey, it will just be a few days. I thought you and your mother were doing the planning. It looked like to me, I was in the way."

Now, those green eyes were flashing like an emerald lying in the sun. "So you are going to leave me defenseless against my mama and her archaic ideas? What am I supposed to do? Will you explain that to me?"

Jack felt like he was sinking in quicksand. No matter what he did or where he reached, he sank deeper in the clinging sand. "I promised Pauly I would help Art. What am I supposed to do?"

Grace stood. "I don't know, Jack. What do you think you should do?"

Jack felt himself sink deeper. "I think I should honor my word to Pauly and Art. They're waiting for me. I figured I could get you to pack some food for me and Art."

Back straight, chin up, and without uttering another word, Grace marched past Jack into the kitchen. He was mystified. What happened? More disturbed than he had ever been before a gunfight, he headed to his room. It took him only a few minutes to pack a change of clothes and grab his rifle. Finished, he stepped into the hallway, closed his door, and headed for the kitchen.

Arriving, he saw two sacks waiting on the table. Grace was busy placing cookies into a smaller bag. She said nothing when he entered. He picked up one of the bags. "I guess these two bags are for us?"

She nodded silently, and Jack waited while she finished with the sack. "This is for the two of you. I made cookies today. You might like them."

Jack took the bag and shoved it into his saddlebags. "Thanks, honey. I'm mighty sorry I upset you. If I hadn't already made a commitment, I wouldn't go." He placed his gear on the table and moved to her. Grasping her arms, he could feel the resistance in her body. She reluctantly turned to him. Once facing him, she wouldn't make eye contact. Jack could feel his patience fading. *I don't have anything to do around here. They ran me out of the house. I don't remember my engagement with Yasmina being like this.*

Suddenly, she threw her arms around his neck and buried her head in his chest. "I'm sorry, too, Jack. I'm such a shrew. I just wanted you to help with the planning so you would be part of it. Your leaving surprised me. I'm so, so sorry." She turned her face up to his.

He kissed the offered lips. Pleasant as they were, he was still bothered by the altercation. "We'll work it out when I get back, Grace. Tell your ma and the boys goodbye for me. I'll be back in a few days." He smiled to her, picked up his equipment and supplies, and headed for the door. Reaching it, a thought sprang to his mind, *My lunch with Casey.* He turned back to Grace. "Honey, I hate to ask you, but I was supposed to have lunch with Casey Carter today, the bank teller. Would you mind dropping by and explaining what happened and that I'll see him when I get back?"

He watched her remove her apron and toss it across a chair. She moved toward the door. Reaching him she smiled, tilted her head back, stood on tiptoe, and gave him a soft kiss. "I'll tell him right now. Have a safe trip, and hurry back to me."

He held open the door for her and watched her glide toward the bank. *What a beautiful and kind woman,* he thought. Jack pulled the door closed and strode toward the stable.

He found Pauly pacing along the front and Art Livingston gone. Pepper was tied at the outside hitching rail. Jack stepped up to his horse, gave him a pat on the neck, fastened his gear, checked the cinch, and stepped into the saddle. "Where's your corral?"

"Down south, just past the school. He said he was going to start them out, and for you to catch up with him. Thanks again, Jack. I know it was short notice."

"No problem. Glad to help. Would you keep an eye on the boys while I'm gone?"

"You bet. See you in a week or so."

Jack touched his hat with his right forefinger and trotted Pepper south, out of Fort Smith.

It's a good thing I'm with Art, Jack thought, breaking out of the forest above a long green valley. *Without him, I would never have found this place.* A log ranch house presided over the breathtaking scene. Art had pulled up, letting the horses graze into the valley.

Jack stopped next to him. "Mighty pretty country."

The rancher nodded in agreement. "I found this place on my way back to East Texas after the war. I was planning on starting a horse ranch back there, but seeing this valley, I figured I'd never find a more beautiful spot. I stopped, and I've been here ever since, going on eleven years now. I'll never get rich here, the valley's too small, but money sure don't matter as long as you have enough."

"True words, Art." Jack watched a man walk out from the barn, shade his eyes, and give a single, sweeping wave before turning and yelling something into the barn.

"That's Blister. He's about the best I've seen with horses. I've always liked those animals, even the hardheads. That's what we raise. We sell most of them in Little Rock, but we have a few buyers who stop by to pick out their own stock."

Two young fellas dashed out of the barn and started running up the slope toward them. Art laughed. "Come on, those are my boys." He jumped his horse into a run, and Jack followed. Reaching the boys, Art slid to a stop and kicked his left foot out of the stirrup. The larger boy handed the smaller one up. Art wrapped his arms around the little man and gave him a squeeze, sitting him on the saddle in front of him. The boy squirmed until he was comfortable, while the older boy shoved his foot in the stirrup and stood facing Art.

"Hi, Pa. You took longer than you said you would."

"I did, didn't I. You miss me?"

The boy grinned. "Nah, Blister kept us busy, and Ma fixed us some pecan pie." His grin widened. "We ate it all."

Art grabbed the boy's hat, yanked it off, and with his knuckles, rubbed his head hard and fast.

Laughing but hurting, the boy grabbed his pa's thick wrist, not even slowing him down. "Stop it, Pa. I'm only kidding. Ma made more than one pie."

The younger boy on the front of the saddle was bouncing up and down, laughing and shouting, "Do me, Pa! Do me! Do me!"

Art shoved his older son's hat on his head crossways and yanked the younger's hat off. This time he was more gentle. Jack sat back, smiling and enjoying the father and sons scene. His mind drifted to first his dead son and then to Billy and Elijah. *I'll enjoy raising those two boys. I'm thinking they might enjoy it, too.*

Art slapped the smaller son's hat back on. "Alright, that's enough. Let's get on down to the house, or your ma's gonna send Blister out after us."

Both boys settled down and said, "Yes, Pa," and the older swung up behind the saddle. Art looked over at Jack. "Would you believe these two unruly curs are mine? This one in back is Aaron, and the one in front is Benjamin. We call him Ben. I tried to name him Beelzebub, but his ma wouldn't let me."

Ben twisted around and frowned at his pa. "You didn't neither."

Art laughed. "No, I sure didn't, son. Boys, this is Mr. Sage. He used to be a United States Marshal."

Jack said, "Howdy, boys."

Aaron spoke first. "You were a marshal, Mr. Sage?"

"I was, but not anymore. I'm just a regular person who's envious of your pa for having such fine-looking sons."

Both the boys grinned, and Art started his horse toward the ranch. He poked Ben. "Aren't you going to say howdy to Mr. Sage?"

Ben turned to look up at his pa, chubby face serious at the reprimand. "I was gonna, Pa, but Aaron was talking, like he always does." Jack was riding a little behind Art and to his left.

Ben turned and leaned past his pa so he could see Jack. "Howdy, Mr. Sage."

"Howdy to you, Benjamin. That's a fine name."

"It is, isn't it? We're named for men from the Bible."

Jack eased Pepper forward so Ben wouldn't have to turn so far. "That's a good place to get names from."

"Yes, sir. That's what Ma says."

A woman stepped from the house and onto the tall porch. She shaded her eyes and watched Art, the boys, and Jack ride into the yard and up to the hitching rail. She had a wide smile on her face. "It's about time you got back. Blister's had his hands full with those three mares. They all foaled in the past two days."

"Hurried as fast as I could, Belle. He nodded to Jack. This here is Mr. Sage. He offered to help herd these wild critters Pauly sold us."

Jack removed his hat. "Morning, ma'am. I'm pleased to meet you. You can call me Jack, if you've a mind."

"Thanks for helping Arthur, Jack. Now get down from there and come in this house. I'll see if I can round up something for you fellers to eat."

"Much obliged. Grace packed food for our trip, but it ran out a couple of days ago." He swung his leg over the saddle and dismounted, holding on to the saddle horn for a minute until his right leg began working again.

Art let Aaron drop to the ground, handed Ben to him, and swung from his horse. "Boys, how about taking these horses to the barn, water and feed them, and give them a good rubdown."

"Yes, sir," Aaron said.

"I'll take Jacob," Ben said.

With their instructions, Aaron stepped to Jack. "I'll be glad to take your horse, Mr. Sage."

"Thank you, Aaron. His name is Pepper. I've got some horse cookies in my saddlebags. Why don't you give him one, and you can also give one to Jacob. In fact, you boys can have one apiece if you like."

Ben made a face. "Horse cookies don't sound that good."

Jack laughed. "You can try a small piece of your brother's. I'm bettin' you'll change your mind."

The two boys headed for the barn with the horses. They passed Blister on his way to the house. He walked straight to Jack and extended his hand. "Name's Wendell Blackman, but everybody calls me Blister. Nice to meet you."

"Jack Sage, Blister." He took the man's hand, and it almost disappeared in his. "It's my pleasure."

At the mention of Jack's name, Blister paused the shake momentarily, looked at Art, then recovered. Art said, "Jack's a *retired* U.S. Marshal. Isn't that right, Jack?"

Jack nodded. "That's a fact, more like an unemployed one. Just a down-and-out old saddle bum."

Everyone laughed at Jack's comment, and Blister visibly relaxed. *I wonder how long he's been dodging the law,* Jack thought. *Well, Blister, you don't have a thing to worry about from me as long as you don't go and try to kill somebody.*

Blister stepped toward Art. "What you want me to do with these new horses?"

Art shook his head. "Leave 'em be for a while. We'll let them rest up a couple of days and then get them branded and start their training."

"We got three foals kicking their heels up in the barn. They're all healthy. One's a mighty pretty fella. Mighty demanding of his mama when he's hungry."

"That's good to know. Sorry for taking so long and leaving you with the whole ranch. I know you must've been busy."

Blister shrugged. "Weren't bad. Belle, she helped a bunch, and the mares did all the work."

"Are you men going to stand out there and jaw or come in here and eat?"

"I already ate," Blister said to Art. "I'm going back to the barn to keep an eye on those mares and foals. I'll talk to you when you're done." Blister nodded to Jack and headed for the barn.

Art motioned to the house. "Come on, big fella, let's go wrap ourselves around some good food."

The two of them had reached the tall porch when Ben stepped out of the barn, called, and pointed up the valley. They both turned. A single horseman was making his way toward the ranch house.

10

Jack watched a single horseman ride down the southern hillside, cross a small stream, and turn his horse toward the ranch house. Art stuck his head inside the doorway. "Honey, it looks like we're going to have another visitor."

"He's not here yet. Get on in here. These eggs are getting cold."

Both men washed at the outside basin. Jack dried his hands and followed Art inside. The house was comfortable. Though some of the furniture looked handmade, it was made by a real craftsman. The table was pecan and as smooth as a young woman's cheek. The color in it was brought out by the natural finish the craftsman had used.

"This is a beautiful table," Jack said. "It's seldom you see this kind of work outside of the city."

"Thanks, I made it. It took me a while, but Belle was willing to put up with the wait."

She walked over and placed her hand on Art's shoulder. "That's because I knew what kind of work he did. Before the war, he worked for my father in his furniture store. That's where we met."

Art placed an arm around his wife's waist and pulled her to him. "It sure is. That was a mighty lucky job." He kissed her on the cheek, and she pushed him away. "We've got guests, Arthur. Act like a gentleman."

The eggs, biscuits, ham, and blackberry jelly looked delicious, but the sound of hoofbeats in the ranch yard brought Art to his feet. "Go ahead and eat, Jack. I've got to see what this feller wants."

Jack gave him a nod, but waited.

Belle tapped the table with a fingernail. "Go ahead, Jack. You don't want this food to get cold. There's nothing you can do, anyway. Dive in."

Jack slid four eggs on his plate and a big slab of ham. He was slicing the ham when he heard Art speak.

"Howdy, mister. How can I help you?"

"I need three horses. Good ones, with bills of sale. I'm willing to pay top dollar."

At the first words from the rider, Jack's hands dropped to his handguns, slipping the restraining loops from the hammers, for he recognized the voice. The last time he had heard that voice was in Cherry Creek, when the man's saloon was shut down. Jack had run him out of town. He glanced at Belle. Her back was to him, and she hadn't seen his quick move. He took a bite of eggs and ham. Jack no longer carried a badge and, in truth, felt no obligation to confront Roman Korkeran, the previous owner of the Gilded Lily, but he wanted to be ready. He chewed the ham and eggs, chasing them with a soft and tasty biscuit.

Art said, "Yes, sir, we can fill your needs. Why don't you take a look at the stock, and after you've decided, we can come up with a price."

Korkeran responded, "They've got to be stayers and fast. I'm not looking for some bag of bones on his last leg. I heard you sold dependable stock, and that's why I rode all the way out here."

"Blister," Art said, "bring up Blaze, Rusty, and Echo. Our

friend can take a look at them. Also bring Star, just in case they don't all satisfy his needs."

"Shore nuff, boss." Moments passed, and a horse was heard galloping from the yard.

Art spoke. "You hungry? Come on in, and grab a bite. We just got in from Fort Smith, driving a new bunch of horses. My wife made us a late breakfast. You're welcome to join us."

"That's friendly of you, mister. I'd like that."

Jack kept on eating. He wanted no violence in this man's home, but there was no time to slip out. The sound of Korkeran's approaching boots carried into the house. Jack made sure both of his hands were above the table. Art stepped through the door, followed by Korkeran. The gambler sauntered into the house, paused to let his eyes adjust, and spotted Jack. There was a flash of recognition but nothing else.

"Howdy, mister," Jack said. "You got here just in time. Mrs. Livingston has fixed a fine meal."

She smiled at Jack, giving him a slight nod. "Why, thank you, sir," and motioned to Korkeran. "Come in, come in. Don't be bashful." She set a plate across from Jack. "Here, have a seat. It's a simple meal, but there's plenty for everyone. My chickens lay more eggs than we're able to eat. I'm glad to see some big appetites."

Korkeran nodded to Belle. "I'm obliged, ma'am," and took the seat across from Jack. The only sign he was surprised was the momentary widening of his eyes, but, Jack thought, *That could have been caused by walking into the darker house.*

Belle began frying more eggs. "There's plenty there, mister. Just help yourself."

Korkeran reached for the platter of eggs. "Thank you, ma'am. It smells delicious."

Jack noticed the gambler's hand as he stretched his arm for the platter. It was steady as a rock. *Good,* he thought, *he's not jumpy. Hopefully, we can get through this without these folk's home getting shot up.* He took another bite of eggs and ham.

Silence reigned at the table while the men ate. In a short time, all three were finishing their last biscuit with fresh butter and blackberry jelly. Jack gently laid his knife alongside the fork on his plate. "Mrs. Livingston, that was a fine meal, especially your jelly, mighty delicious. I thank you."

"You're quite welcome, Mr. Sage. I enjoy feeding hungry men."

"Yes, ma'am," Korkeran said, "I want to add my thanks. I had no idea when I rode up here today that I'd get surprised with such a delicious treat." Korkeran was staring at Jack when he spoke. Jack couldn't help but allow a slight grin to drift across his mouth.

"You are most welcome, sir. Come again, anytime."

The sound of horses drifted into the house. Art stood. "Well, mister, it sounds like the horses are arriving, if you're ready."

Belle frowned at her husband and spoke to Korkeran. "Sir, I've just made a fresh pot of coffee. Can't you join Mr. Sage for a cup before you leave?"

It was all Jack could do to keep from rolling his eyes. *Leave him alone, Belle,* he thought. *Let him leave. You have no idea of the threat this man brings. If we met on a street, we'd probably be shooting. At least he would. For me, it's in the past.*

Korkeran shook his head. "No, thanks, ma'am. It smells tantalizing, but I must look at these horses and be on my way." He turned to Jack. "Mr. Sage, perhaps we'll have the pleasure another time."

Jack mixed his coffee. "I look forward to it, Mr. Korkeran. You have a good day."

Blister pulled up with the three horses, and Art motioned to Korkeran. "They're here."

"Certainly." Korkeran headed for the door, stopped, and gave a nod to Belle. "Ma'am, I thank you," and he was gone.

Jack let out a long breath and took another sip of coffee while he listened to the men dickering over a price. Art drove a hard bargain. He was asking five hundred dollars for each horse. At last, they came to an agreement. Korkeran paid Art thirteen hundred and fifty dollars for the three, and Jack listened with relief as Korkeran galloped from the ranch yard with the horses.

Art came back in to a smiling wife. He looked across the room and held up the money. She came across the dining room, took the money, and stepped into a back room. After pouring himself a cup of coffee, and one for his wife, the horse rancher took his place at the head of the table. "Those little transactions help the coffers."

Jack smiled. "I just bet they do. You drive a hard bargain."

Art grinned. "I learned from the best, my pa. He was one of the finest horse traders I ever knew. I guess a little of it rubbed off on me."

Belle returned, smiling. She walked up to her husband, leaned over, grasped his head, and gave him a big kiss on the cheek. "I told Papa you were the man for me. He just couldn't stand me marrying a furniture maker. His life had been so hard, but I told him you'd take care of me and however many kids we had."

At her last statement, her face took on a momentary sadness. She poured herself coffee and sat next to her husband. He patted her hand and then squeezed it. Belle looked across at Jack. "Sorry, our third child, a little girl, was stillborn, and the doctor said we can't have any more. I should be happy with the boys we have, but I had so wanted a large family."

Jack shook his head. "Sorry, ma'am. Losing a child is a terrible loss, and not being able to have more must also be mighty bad."

She brightened, though Jack could see it was forced. "Yes, but we have two fine boys and this beautiful place, for which we are mightily thankful. Isn't it pretty here, Jack?"

"Yes, ma'am, this is a pretty place. I'm thinking you two are mighty lucky people."

Blister called from the yard, "Hey, Art. You about done in there? The boys and I want you to take a look at these foals."

Belle jumped to her feet. "Oh, yes." She grabbed her husband's arm and pulled him erect. "Let's go look at the foals. Would you like to see them, Jack?"

"I sure would, ma'am. It would please me to see those little fellas, but I best be on my way."

Art's forehead wrinkled in dismay. "You're not leaving now? We just got here. You and your horse need to rest up. At least let me show you around, Jack. You can leave in the morning if you must."

Jack shook his head. "No, I've got to get on out of here. I may have brought trouble on you folks. You see, I knew that Korkeran fella who bought your horses. We had a little trouble a few years ago. He swore he'd kill me if he ever saw me again. I'm mighty sorry for bringing this down on you, but if I get out of here, maybe he'll leave you folks alone."

Art shook his head. "He won't bother us. I don't ask a man questions when I sell him a horse, and I have some of the best horses in the country. My clients come from all different types of folks, if you get my drift. No one bothers us, from either side of the law. You needn't worry about us, Jack. We'll be fine, but like I said, you and your horse need to rest up."

Jack shook his head. "We'll take it easy going back, but we'd better go, just in case. Pepper's got himself a good rubdown and a bite of feed, and I've just had myself a fine meal." He grinned at Belle. "I'm much obliged, Belle."

The three of them had walked out onto the tall porch. Jack looked across the valley. "Yes, sir, this is a fine-looking place. I envy you folks."

"There's land all over, Jack. It just depends on the kind you want. Lots of folks have gone to Texas. That's where I was headed when I saw this valley. You might look around over there."

"I just might."

Aaron, the Livingstons' oldest son, stepped out from the barn door and waved. "Ma, Pa, hurry and come see the foals."

"We're coming, son," Art replied. "Keep your pants on."

Jack laughed. "Looks like you two are wanted in the barn. I'll go with you and take a look, then I've got to hit the trail." The three of them descended the steps and headed across the yard to the barn.

~

THE TRAIL back to Fort Smith had been uneventful for Jack. Once he had the feeling he was being followed, but he saw and heard nothing, so he put it aside as being edgy. Thoughts of Grace had pushed Korkeran from his mind. The afternoon sun was drifting lower when he rode up the main street of Fort Smith. Several people waved or spoke to him as he walked Pepper along the street. The town was busy, but the warm weather was holding. If it stayed like this, trees would start budding out, and those buds were going to get nipped when the temperatures dropped below freezing again, which they would.

Pauly's voice called from deep in the darkness of the barn as Jack approached. "That didn't take long."

Jack rode Pepper into the barn and saw Pauly mucking out one of the stalls. He had stopped and was leaning on his shovel. "How'd it go?"

Swinging down from his saddle, Jack said, "No problem. Art has a nice place."

"That he does."

"Everything alright around here?"

"Had a little excitement while you were gone."

Jack's mind dashed to Grace and the boys.

Pauly must have seen the concern, for he said, “Don’t worry, Grace and the kids are fine. This was law stuff.”

Jack shook his head. “Pauly, you know I’m done with that.”

Pauly nodded. “I know, but you’ll want to know about this. Marshal Berry’s been shot.”

Jack jerked around from Pepper. “How is he?”

“Bad, Jack. He took one in the back last night while he was making the rounds. They don’t have any idea who might have done it. He’s hanging on, but according to the doc, things don’t look good for him.”

Jack shook his head. *In the back,* he thought, *a man can’t protect himself from back-shooters, especially at night. Too bad, Strawn is a good man.* “Pauly, would you take care of Pepper? I’ve got to see Grace.”

“Sure, Jack.”

Trail dust filled the deep creases across his forehead. He was concerned about Strawn, but also Grace. She had lost her first husband to the war. Now, even though he had quit the law business, Jack felt sure Grace carried fears about him and possible retribution. Jack pushed the door open, stepped inside, laid his hat and saddlebags on a table, and stood his rifle in a corner. He stopped for a moment, listening. There were noises coming from the kitchen. *Probably getting ready for supper,* Jack thought. He strode into the kitchen to see Matthew over the stove and Grace rolling out dough on the table.

Before she looked up, he could see worry etched across her lovely face. Her brow was wrinkled, the laugh lines at the corners of her eyes were pulled down, and she pursed her lips. Grace glanced up. Seeing him, everything changed. Her brow smoothed, the laugh wrinkles turned up, and her red lips stretched in a wide smile.

She rushed to wipe her hands on her apron, and hurried around the table to him, lifting her face as she neared. “Oh, Jack, I am glad to see you. I missed you so. I’m sor—”

He took her in his arms and pressed his lips to hers. The warmth of her filled him with joy. He had missed her. An argument meant nothing.

Two pairs of running feet stopped. "Oh, man. They're kissin' again."

Jack could feel Grace's lips grin against his. She pulled away. He looked at the hallway door to see Elijah and Billy staring, a look of disgust on each face. Billy worse than Elijah. "How are you boys doing?"

The disgust vanished, and they broke into grins. They both said, "Good." Then Elijah elbowed Billy, who said, "Mr. Sage, do you remember offering to take us shooting?"

Jack gave the boys a nod. "I sure do. If you boys get your chores done in time, we might take a little jaunt to the river this evening and blast a few limbs. How does that sound?"

Elijah held his hand out, palm down. "Look how steady my hand is, Mr. Sage."

"Like a rock, son. You two best get busy. I want to leave right after supper, before dark." With raised eyebrows, he gave Grace a questioning look.

She smiled at the two boys, who stood, breath held, waiting for her pronouncement. "You two get moving if you're going to get your chores done first." The rest she said was to fast-retiring young backs. "And don't forget to milk those cows. We need their milk."

The boys glanced back, and Billy called, "We won't forget, Ma." They slammed through the back door and were gone.

She stepped away from Jack, her hands drifting down to his biceps, and her face growing serious. "I am so glad you're back. Did you hear about Strawn?"

"Yeah, Pauly said the doc doesn't hold out much hope."

Grace nodded. "He's dying. I'm so glad you gave up your badge." She looked over her shoulder at Matthew, then back at Jack. "Shall we talk in the parlor?"

Jack nodded. "Sure, but I'm covered in trail dust."

Grace took his arm. "You'll be fine." She glanced over her shoulder. "Matthew, if you need me, I'll be in the parlor."

"I think we're fine, madam. I'll finish the bread and get it in the oven. Don't you worry about a thing." He glanced at Jack. "Welcome back, Mr. Sage."

"Thanks, Matthew. I won't keep her long."

"She deserves some rest. She's been working solid since you left. If it isn't cooking, it's sweeping or cleaning."

Jack looked at Grace as they entered the parlor and sat on the loveseat. "How is Mary?"

She shrugged and rolled her eyes. "I don't know, Jack. I'm sure she's fine, but all Mama can think about is this wedding. She's like a general marshaling her troops. All of her friends are busy getting everything ready. It looks like Reverend Beeson will perform the ceremony. Is that alright with you?"

He shook his head. "Grace, I don't care. I just want to get it done."

She smiled and leaned her head against his chest. "So do I. Who would think it would turn into such a production?"

He had wrapped an arm around her. "Have you thought about after the wedding? For the honeymoon, we can travel anywhere, even Europe, if you like."

She giggled into his chest. "Europe, my goodness. I never thought there would be any possibility of ever seeing Paris."

"If that's what you want, Grace, it's yours. We can take a couple of months and travel the Continent. You have Matthew to help Mary. She can look after the boys."

Grace jerked up and stared at Jack. "You're serious?"

"Sure." He chuckled, a big grin stretching his stubble-covered face. "We probably wouldn't even be missed."

Jack was enjoying dreaming with his future bride. It was the first time he realized he was truly free. The cost of a trip to Europe, for the two of them, would barely put a dent in the money he had received so far. *It would be fun,* he thought, *showing Grace the places he'd been and enjoying her excitement when seeing them for the first time.* He watched her, thinking about it.

Finally, she shook her head. "Jack, that is too extravagant for now. Let's save it for later, when we're older and the boys are grown with their own wives and children. That will be the time for us to be a little extravagant. Right now, I'd like to see us build something. Have you thought about what you'd like to do?"

11

His gray eyes brightened. "I have, honey. There's a place in Texas. I was once a town marshal there. I'd love to start a horse and cattle ranch in that country. Build it so the boys would have a place where they could grow into good, strong men."

She was watching his face, her green eyes delving into his. "Oh, Jack, it sounds wonderful. I've always had a secret urge to go to Texas. I just like the sound of it. Texas. It sounds big and strong, like you."

Jack grinned, feeling his heart leap. His future bride liked the idea of a ranch. "I'm not that big or strong, and it'll be hard, Grace. Texas can be hot and dusty. It's still a place where outlaws congregate, where there's little law except a gun and a rope, but it's changing, and we can be a part of that change." His voice had risen with his enthusiasm.

"What change would that be?"

Grace turned to see her mother, who had just entered the boardinghouse. "Come in, Mama. We're discussing our plans after the wedding."

"Oh, how nice," Mary replied, with little enthusiasm. She

entered the parlor and dropped into the green wingback. "Where is this you two want to be part of a change?"

Jack leaned toward Mary. "Texas. I was telling Grace I've been over a lot of different country from Texas to Wyoming. There's a small town a ways west of Austin. At least it was small when I was there several years ago. It has a nice creek running through it. It would be a wonderful place to start a ranch."

Mary's eyebrows arched. "You're talking about taking my daughter and grandsons to Texas and leaving me here to run this?" She held her arms wide, palms up.

"No, ma'am, I'm not. I'm talking about all of us going. Becoming a part of a growing state. Putting our brand on that country. Why, it would be a place where those boys and any others who might come along could grow into men."

When Jack spoke of more sons, Grace wrapped an arm around his. "You hadn't mentioned that before."

He smiled at her. "I have now. How do you feel about it?"

She returned his smile. "I like it." Then she turned to Mary. "Oh, Mama, come with us. You can watch your grandsons and maybe granddaughters grow and start families of their own. It will be wonderful."

Mary's face remained serious. "So, Grace, what do we do with Ma's Board and Eats?"

Grace leaned toward her mother and lowered her voice. "I believe Matthew would buy it for the right price. I have said nothing to him, but he's made several comments that indicate he might be interested."

Mary's eyes widened. "Really? I thought he said he wanted to continue to Santa Fe."

Grace shrugged. "He likes Fort Smith. I think there is a good chance he would buy it."

Mary leaned back in her chair. "That does put a different face on it, but do you two really want an old woman tagging along with you?"

Jack gave a single laugh. "You're not old, Mary, and you are in a lot better shape than some folks I've seen heading west, and you will be a great support to your daughter and grandsons. We more than want you. We need you."

Mary clasped her hands together. "Jack, you have made an old woman feel wanted. Let me think about it."

"Don't think too long, Mama." Grace looked up at her husband. "Our honeymoon may be spent on the way to Texas."

"Nope," Jack said, a big smile on his face. "We'll at least take the riverboat to Little Rock and spend a couple of days there. Then we'll go to Texas."

Grace shrugged. "I guess my future husband has decided, but after Little Rock, we'll be off for Texas, and Mama, we want you with us."

Jack put his arm around Grace and hugged her to him. "But Mary, I've got to know when you're going to let me marry your daughter. This mystery is driving me crazy, and I need to make sure they've got room for us on the riverboat."

Mary laughed. "Oh, Jack, I am so glad you finally got back. We have been bursting to tell you. How does April the first sound to you?"

Jack frowned. "It sounds like a long way off. I'm ready to get this done."

Mary shook her head. "But there is so much to do. So many people are working to pull this together. It will be wonderful, but to make it that way, it takes a little time." Her tone changed to that of a mother chiding a child. "Don't be so impatient, Jack. You'll be married for a long time."

Before he could respond, Billy and Elijah charged into the room. "We're done, Ma." They looked at Jack. "You ready to go?"

Grace grabbed Billy by both arms. "Slow down. Did you feed the chickens?"

Elijah almost shouted. "We did!"

"What about the milk cows?"

Billy grinned. "Milked, and the buckets are covered and cooling in the back room." He looked at Jack. "You're ready, right?"

Grace still held Billy. "He's tired, boys. Jack has traveled a long way."

Both of the boys groaned. "You promised, Mr. Sage."

"Alright, boys, but there's a question you have to answer first."

Grace released Billy, and both he and Elijah turned to Jack.

"Do you mind if I marry your ma?"

Both sets of eyes grew wide, then grins split their faces. Billy spoke first. "Does that mean we won't have to see all that kissing? It's kinda disgusting."

Jack reached out and grabbed Billy. "Boy, did I ever count your ribs?" His big fingers started going up Billy's ribs like his pa's had traveled over his.

Billy broke out laughing and squirming. "Stop, I don't mind. Stop!"

Jack jerked the boy to him and gave him a huge hug, then he grabbed Elijah and did the same with him. Both boys were beside themselves with laughter. When they calmed down, Jack asked them again. "Seriously, boys, now tell me the truth. Are you alright with me marrying your ma?"

The boys grew solemn. Billy spoke first. "Mr. Sage, I'd be pleased if you married my ma, as long as I could call you pa."

Jack nodded. "You'd make me proud if you did, Billy, but I want you to know one thing. I'm not trying to take the place of your real pa. No one can do that. You understand me?"

The boy gave a nod, and Jack turned to Elijah. "What about you, Elijah? How do you feel about your ma and me getting hitched?"

"I really like the idea, Mr. Sage, and I'd like to call you pa, too. Can I start now?"

The question caught Jack off guard. He looked at Grace, who

gave him a tiny shrug. “Elijah, I don’t see anything wrong with you calling me pa.”

The boy grinned at Billy. “Then, Pa, can we go shooting?”

Jack let out a laugh. “You boys don’t give up, do you?”

“No, sir,” was shouted in unison.

He stood. “Then let’s go see if we can burn some powder. What do you want to shoot?”

Billy said, “Your revolvers.”

Jack looked down at the younger boy. “Well, Elijah, what would you like to shoot?”

He looked up with a grin. “Everything.”

“You might miss supper.”

Elijah shook his head. “We don’t care.”

Grace stood, laughing. “We’ll see about that, but mentioning supper, I better get busy. Folks will be showing up soon.”

Jack rose with Grace, put his arm around her, and gave her a squeeze. Then he bent and planted a kiss on Mary’s cheek. “Having you with us makes the family whole.” He straightened, strode to the Winchester, picked it up, and reached for the door latch. The boys were right behind him, but before he could pull, the door opened to Deputy Marshal Buck Walker.

His face was somber. “Marshal Berry’s dead.”

Jack felt the sadness come over him. He had gotten to know the marshal well. They had gone through tough times together, and now he was dead. “I’m mighty sorry, Buck. He was a good man.”

“He sure was. His death is a real loss to this town and Judge Bell.”

Jack said nothing.

Finally, Buck spoke again. “Judge Bell would like to see you.”

With the loss of Marshal Berry, Jack could not bring himself to refuse the judge’s request. He looked down at the long faces of Billy and Elijah.

Elijah nodded. "You go ahead, Pa. We can shoot another time."

Billy extended his hand. "Marshal Berry was always nice to us. We'll put your Winchester in your room."

Jack handed the rifle to Billy. "Be careful."

In unison, they said, "We will," and marched sedately along the hallway to Jack's room.

Jack watched them for a moment, then turned to Buck, who had a questioning look on his face. "Pa?"

"Why not? Grace and I are getting married. Let's go."

Arriving at the judge's office, Nesbit waved them through the open door. The judge was sitting behind his desk, surrounded by several stacks of papers and books. He looked up and rose as they entered. "Thanks, Buck. Would you gather the deputies in the courtroom? I'll be there shortly."

Buck nodded and exited, pulling the door closed behind him.

Judge Bell pointed to one of the chairs in front of his desk. "Have a seat, Jack. Thank you for coming."

The two men lowered themselves into their respective chairs, and the judge leaned back. "It's a sad day today. I've known Strawn Berry for quite a while. He was a no-nonsense, honest lawman. He is going to be missed by this community."

"He was a good marshal, Judge," Jack said. "Do you have any idea who shot him?"

"No. There wasn't any evidence around the scene. I'm afraid this is one of those shocking crimes that go unpunished. It galls me, but that's the way it is."

Jack shook his head. "I'm sorry to hear that. You know when they'll be having Strawn's funeral?"

"No, I haven't spoken to his wife, but as warm as the weather's been, I suspect it will be soon." The judge cleared his throat. "I had another reason for asking you up here today, Jack."

Jack said nothing.

"First, there's this." He handed an envelope, with the stamp of the presidential seal, to Jack. "It arrived today."

Jack took the envelope and examined it. It contained an object he recognized instantly by the feel. "I haven't seen Schofield around."

"He returned to Washington the same day you left. There has been no contact, either with him or the president, except for this single letter to you. I'd appreciate you reading it now, if you don't mind. It might bear on the subject I'd like to discuss with you." The judge handed a letter opener to Jack.

After taking it, he slipped it under the flap and drew it across. The opener was sharp, leaving a smooth edge on the severed paper. He tilted the envelope, allowing his badge to fall into his hand. He placed it on the judge's desk and pulled out three sheets of paper. Jack immediately recognized the tilted scrawl of the president, though the words were clear and precise. He took only a short time reading the contents. Finished, he handed the pages across to the judge. "I don't think the president would mind you reading this."

Jack waited as the judge read the letter, shaking his head at the end. "It amazes me that Carter could have let his personal feelings take over, but I can understand the president's thinking as far as the senator is concerned."

He handed the letter back across the desk to Jack, who refolded it, slid the sheets inside the envelope, and placed the envelope inside an inner vest pocket.

The judge gazed at Jack. "So, I don't think we'll be seeing Carter again."

Jack nodded. "That's a good thing. I don't care how close he was to the senator's family or Sean Harris. He had no right to instigate the killing of Reno Flint and use me as the instrument. Though a gambler, Reno was a good man."

The judge placed his elbows on the arms of his chair and steepled his fingers. Over his fingertips, he examined Jack. "I know you are planning to marry Grace. Congratulations. She is a wonderful and beautiful woman, and I believe you are a fortunate man. Does this letter from the president cause any changes in the plans you have laid?"

Jack held the no longer shiny and unblemished star Carter Schofield had given to him in New Mexico. Scratches and dents from wear and blows he had taken dulled the original luster. *It's like me,* he thought, *no longer bright and shiny, but still effective.*

He looked over the badge at Bell, thinking, *This is a courageous man. With the help of his marshals, he is cleaning up this territory. Good men are needed out here to control the vermin who roam the hills and valleys, but I'm no longer one of them.* "Judge, the president has made a generous offer, allowing me to remain a marshal-at-large, under my discretion. I suspect I'll accept his offer, but this decision affects more people than just myself. I'll be talking it over with Grace, and after considering the good and the bad of the offer, we will make a decision, so I won't know what I've decided until later."

The judge didn't immediately respond, but rocked back and forth several times, his steepled fingers resting in the space below his bottom lip.

Jack said nothing.

Finally, he stopped. "Jack, I need help. With Strawn killed, I need a marshal in charge of this bunch. I have the authority to make that appointment."

Jack nodded. "Buck is young, but of the deputies I've met, I think he's the best you've got."

Judge Bell nodded. "I agree with you. Buck has learned a lot from Strawn and you, and he is the best I have, but none of these men have learned how to manage other men. That's what Strawn was good at. He knew his men and knew who to send where, or which deputy to send after which outlaw or outlaws. That's why I need you."

Jack slipped the badge into a vest pocket, and his big hands dropped to the arms of his chair. Head shaking, he rose.

"Jack, just wait. Sit down, and hear me out."

"Judge, I'm done, finished. I'm not chasing men any longer. I'll not take the chance of killing another innocent man. If I have to pull a gun, it'll be to protect me or my family, not to bring a man to justice."

Jack had risen to his full height.

The judge shook his head. "Jack, sit down, please. Hear me out."

The huge lawman remained standing, thinking, *It is time for me to be out of here. I want to take Grace, Mary, and the boys and head for Texas. I'm tired of being the person people turn to when they need a mess cleaned up.* He found himself slowly dropping into the chair. His body was doing what his conscious mind was against. "I'm not your man, Judge."

"Hear me out. This won't be a permanent thing. I just need some time to get past the loss of Strawn and decide about who can fill his shoes."

"How much time do you need?"

In frustration, the judge shook his head. "I don't know, Jack. How long does it take to find a good man?"

"You've got good men surrounding you right now. You mentioned Buck, and there's also Nesbit. He's older, less likely to go off half-cocked. I'd say he's an excellent man."

"I've thought about him, Jack, but he's been in this office for quite a while. He hasn't been out in the field."

"Alright, Judge. If you want me to stay, you've got to give me a length of time, and then I'm going to discuss it with Grace, a month, two?"

The judge shook his head again. "I was thinking more along the line of the rest of the year."

Jack rose again. "Then you're thinking along the wrong line. I'll talk to Grace, but you'd better be adjusting your thinking to more like a month, or two at the most. Now, don't you have a bunch of marshals waiting for you in your courtroom?"

Judge Bell stood. "Yes, could you attend?"

"No."

The judge slammed his pen back into the well. "You are the hardest man I know to get along with. I just need you there for a few minutes."

Jack shook his head. "No, you don't, Judge. You want me there so you can persuade me to stay. There is no persuasion that will work on me. I'm going to talk to Grace this evening. She's serving supper right now, so she'll be busy. When she's done, we'll sit down and discuss the possibility of my staying for a short time. So, for now, I'm out of here. Have a good meeting."

Jack yanked the judge's door open and charged out, closing it behind him. He glanced at Leon Nesbit, who sat behind his desk, grinning. Still irritated at the judge trying to persuade him to go to the marshal meeting, Jack snapped at Nesbit, "What are you grinning at?"

"You made me two bucks."

Jack stopped. "How's that?"

Nesbit's grin widened. "Buck and I had a little wager. I bet you'd come out of the judge's office mad, and he said both of you were in good moods, and it wouldn't happen." He held up two fingers. "Two bucks."

Jack glared at the deputy for a moment longer, then shook his head. "It seems we strike sparks."

Still grinning, Nesbit said, "Every time."

A corner of Jack's mouth lifted. "I'm glad someone is profiting from it."

Nesbit grew serious. "You gonna be our new boss, Jack? Every man would love for you to say yes."

Without thinking, Jack said, "How'd you know about it?"

Nesbit held his thumb and forefinger close together, almost touching. "Thin walls."

Jack turned and, for the first time, gave the outside of the judge's office a close look. "Then you know you're in the running. Don't you want the job?"

Nesbit shook his head. "The judge is right. I've been out of the field for quite a while. I'm happy right where I am. I get to see my wife and kids every night, and most nights, I get to eat supper with them. Why would I want to give that up? Besides, Buck is a fire-eater. If you're not going to do it, he's the man for the job. Oh, there's some of the older marshals who might be put off for a while, but they'll come around, and as far as experience, we were all inexperienced at one time. You learn by doing."

"You know, Leon, I think you're right on both counts." He glanced at the judge's office. "Don't let the judge keep those boys waiting too long. I'll see you later." He turned and headed for the stairs.

Nesbit spoke to his back as he strode away. "Take the job, Jack. We need you, at least for a while."

12

Jack and Grace sat alone in the parlor. The family and the guests had retired for an early start the next day. He felt the desperation in her warm hands clasping him in a tight grip.

"Oh, Jack. I just want you to be done with the law. It seems lawmen don't retire, they get buried, and I don't want that happening to you."

He gave her a slight grin. "That makes two of us. I want us both to live long and happy lives. However, the offer from the president allows me a lot of leeway. I can keep the authority without taking orders. It could help us in the future. We wouldn't have to brook interference from local law."

"It sounds good, Jack, and it might be. It could be a wonderful gift from the president, but it could also be his method of keeping you tied to him so he could call on you anytime he felt like it."

Jack rubbed a tough, calloused thumb along the back of Grace's soft hand. "You could be right, but he'll have to act quick. This is the end of his second term. Whoever wins the election will probably appoint their own marshals. When they see me in Texas, doing my own thing, I'll probably be fired. You can bet on it, so, honey, he's only got the rest of this year, and, should he attempt it, I'll quit."

The lamp cast shadows across Grace, turning her green eyes black. Jack felt they were probing into his soul. She leaned nearer to him. "But what about the judge and his request? How do you answer him? We have our wedding coming up on the first of April, less than a month away. What are you going to do?"

Jack leaned toward her, gazing into those dark eyes. "What would you like me to do?"

She shook her head, loosening her hair. Deep black locks tumbled over her shoulders. "Oh, I don't know. The judge has been really good to us. After Papa died, Mama explained to him her idea of a boardinghouse, and he helped us purchase this building, and look at how he pushed through Elijah's adoption. I feel like we owe him."

Jack nodded. "The job will be primarily administrative. I'm going to be keeping the marshal's office running and giving Buck a few more pointers. The judge feels like he needs a little more direction before taking the job. He's ready right now, but there are a few more things I can show him."

Concern filled her eyes. "Jack, I don't want you shot in the back like Strawn."

He shook his head. "That won't be happening. I hope he tries. I'm onto him. The man likes to get close, and that'll be his undoing. You don't need to be worried, honey."

She gave a long sigh. "How long do you think?"

"If we wait and plan our departure for the fifteenth of May, we'll be well past the cold weather and most of the rain except for a stray thunderstorm. A departure in May should put us arriving at Cherry Creek no later than the middle of July. There should still be sufficient water along the way. If we wait until later, that will put us into the end of July and August. We'd have less chance of finding water. I'd leave the judge's service on the day of our wedding, the first day of May, and we'd have the next two weeks to go to Little Rock on our honeymoon."

The mention of their honeymoon brought a smile to her lips. She raised her left hand and softly stroked his cheek, her fingers feeling soft along his thick stubble. "Oh, Jack. I can't believe we're making such plans. I love you so much."

He placed his big hand over hers. "I love you too, Grace. I'm a lucky man." They leaned toward each other, and Jack felt the warmth of her breath as her soft lips touched his. Moments passed, and he felt the blood coursing through his body. He pulled away. "I think we best be cautious."

She shrugged. "What's to be cautious about? We only have Mama, the boys, and twelve guests who might barge in."

He grinned. "True. Now what about the May date?"

"Yes, May the first sounds good to me. Mama may squawk about changing the wedding date, but I promise you, she'll be secretly relieved that she has longer to prepare. She'll also love a May wedding."

She leaned toward him again. Suddenly, a single gunshot barked from outside.

Jack leaped to his feet and yanked the revolver from his left holster. "Take this. Be careful. It has a sensitive trigger."

Grace was also standing. "I know how to use it, Jack. Go find out what happened."

He grabbed his hat from the rack, opened the front door, looked both ways, and stepped onto the boardwalk, pulling the door closed behind him. With weapon in hand, he closed the door and started for the gathering crowd, just three buildings away.

Jack scanned the surrounding areas. All was dark except for the light streaming from buildings where doors were jerked open. Outlines of men with rifles were seen in those doorways, ready to shoot at something. *This is a perfect opportunity for neighbor to shoot neighbor,* Jack thought. He reached into his pocket and grasped the badge, shoving it into its familiar position. After locking the pin into the small clasp, Jack used his empty left hand to move people out of his way.

"Move aside, folks. Let me by." With his size and the authority in his voice, the bystanders jumped to obey. They made a path to the man lying on his back. The badge on the left side of his vest glinted in the light.

A young feminine voice pleaded at the edge of the crowd, "Please let me by. Let me by."

The deputy who rolled the dead man over saw Jack, stood, and stepped to his side. "The lady is his wife. They've been married less than a year."

Jack dropped his revolver into its holster and moved through the crowd to the young woman's side. "Ma'am, I'm Marshal Sage. Let me help you." He placed his arm around her shoulders and commanded, "Clear the way."

Sensing the drama of the moment, the crowd had gone silent, and all could hear the woman's whispered voice. "Is it Rory?"

Moving her through the separating crowd, Jack spoke softly. "Ma'am, I didn't know him, but one of the other deputies says it is. I'm sorry."

Before reaching the dark form of the young deputy, the girl began to cry. Several people held lanterns high, illuminating his pale face. The young woman fell to her knees next to her husband and pressed herself to his dead body. "No, oh no. Rory, please don't be dead. Why is this happening? Oh, Rory." She broke into a wail and tried to lift him to her.

Jack bent and gently but firmly lifted her, breaking her grip on her dead husband.

She continued to wail, "Oh, Rory, please don't leave me."

Another woman, who was the appropriate age to be her mother, pushed through the crowd, nodded to Jack, and wrapped a shawl around her daughter. "Come, Linda, come home with us.

Your father will see to Rory." She was able to guide her daughter away, but the girl continued to cry and call for her husband.

Deputies now surrounded the crowd. Jack saw the large exit wound in Rory's chest. The deputy who had turned the body was standing next to him. "Did you or anyone else see anything?"

The young man had a slow drawl. "No, Marshal. I ain't seen a thing, and I was the first to get here, but there weren't nary a movement other than folks rushing out of their homes. Rory was stretched out, facedown, with a big hole in his back. He was dead before he hit the ground." The deputy nodded at the dead man. "Look at the blood. That bullet had to go right through the middle of his heart. Whoever shot him was serious." The young man stopped, holding his head up and sniffing. "I noticed one thing. The smell of black powder was strong. I'm thinking whoever shot him had to be in the alley, maybe close to him. I'm guessing right behind him."

The smoke and gunpowder smell still hung in the air. There was little breeze to move it out of the alley. *So whoever is doing this is getting close,* Jack thought. *The shooter wants the pleasure of being almost on top of his victim when he pulls the trigger.* Jack pointed to one man with a lantern. "Come over here." To the deputy, he said, "Help me turn him over, gently. I want to see the bullet entry."

The deputy was careful. They lifted the dead man's body, rotated him, and gently laid him facedown on the ground. The man holding the lantern stepped close. "Lift the lantern higher," Jack said, "where it's out of my eyes, but shining on this young fella's back."

The man moved closer and lifted the lantern above Jack's head and over the body. Jack could see the darkened and burned circle around the bullet hole in the deputy's shirt-back. His mind raced as he examined the body. *The killer had his weapon less than an inch away from Rory's back when he pulled the trigger. He might even have gotten blood splatters on his clothing and boots.* He motioned the deputy close and whispered, "How many deputies do you think we have in the crowd?"

The man straightened and looked around, then dropped back close to Jack. "Marshal, I'd say there must be five or six."

"Good. I'll give you a minute to let them know, but I want you to tell the men to surround the crowd and keep everyone here. I want each person examined." He looked at the open door of the adjacent building, above which a sign hung: Attorney at Law. "Bring them into this law office, and we'll check them for gunpowder and blood. No one is to leave until each is checked."

The deputy nodded. "What about the women, Marshal? You want they should be allowed to go home?"

Jack thought back to the time a woman with a gun almost killed him. If he hadn't stumbled, he wouldn't be here today. "We'll check them, too."

"Marshal, that ain't gonna sit well with these folks. There's wives, mothers, and daughters in this crowd. Their menfolk can be mighty protective."

"We're not going to strip them. We're going to check their clothing for blood or visible powder residue. Now go ahead, get the men spread out. I'll speak to the crowd."

Jack rose, and the deputy began moving through the crowd, stopping at each deputy as he came to him. Jack saw a few head shakes, but everyone followed his orders. He addressed the people, motioning to the building he had showed to the deputy. "Whose office is this?"

A middle-aged man stepped forward, dressed in a plush robe over his pajamas. "It is mine, Marshal. I am Archibald Miller, an attorney."

The crowd, curious why Jack was asking Miller about his office, grew silent, listening.

"If you don't mind, Mr. Miller, I'll need to use your office for a while. It won't be long. If you'll light any additional lamps you have inside, I would appreciate it."

The lawyer hesitated. "I do mind, Marshal." He turned and pointed across the street to the marshal's office. "Why don't you use your office? It's just across the street."

"Mr. Miller, the court will reimburse you for the use, and we won't take too long. Now, please step inside and light your lamps."

Judge Bell stepped into the light. "If I may, Marshal." He turned to the crowd. "Folks, I'm sorry it must be under such terrible circumstances, but Marshal Sage has accepted my request to take over Marshal Berry's position."

A murmur spread through the crowd. Judge Bell turned back to Jack. "Marshal Sage, Mr. Miller is a member of the court and brings up a valid point about your office. Couldn't you conduct whatever you have in mind there?"

"No, Judge, I can't, and I don't have time for a debate." His head turned to the attorney. "Mr. Miller, get those lamps lit now!"

The attorney puffed up like a swollen bullfrog and was about to respond to Jack's order, but the marshal no longer faced him. He had turned to the crowd.

Jack noted his deputies had surrounded the people and stood ready to stop anyone who tried to leave. He began. "Folks, I need your help. I want to speak to, and examine the clothing of each one of you, individually, in Mr. Miller's office. It will only take a moment, but I ask you to remain here until we've talked. That includes women and men."

A man close to the front of the crowd, whose wife stood next to him, stepped forward. "Marshal, you ain't examining my wife now or ever. You can—"

In two steps, Jack was within arm's reach of the man. "What's your name?"

"I'm Bill Wakely, and I own the feed and grain store."

Jack knew his size alone intimidated most people. Coupled with the badge, he usually could control most situations without violence. He was glad Wakely had spoken up. It gave him an opportunity to quiet this man and others who might have the same concerns. In his most considerate and persuasive voice, Jack began. "Mr. Wakely, let me assure you, we have the utmost respect for you and Mrs. Wakely. Allow me to explain what we're doing. It appears young Rory was shot in the back from very close range. It may have been close enough for the killer to have gunpowder or blood on his or her clothing. That is what we're checking for. There will be no disrespect of any kind of your wife. I give you my word on that." He touched his hat to Mr. Wakely's wife.

Mr. Wakely said, "Marshal, do you actually believe that whoever committed the murder of Rory Stewart would stand around in this crowd?"

"Sir, I believe it is possible. Quite often, killers like to observe the harm and shock their brutality causes."

A voice lifted near Jack. "Marshal Sage, you don't know me, but I'm Barnes Olson. I own the newspaper. Please let me add my most emphatic testimony to your statement." He turned to the crowd. "Friends, the marshal speaks the truth. It's all about psychology, which I won't go into here, but killers love hurting people, and even more, they love the mayhem they cause. They also like the notoriety, so what the marshal says is fact. The killer could be standing next to you right now."

The newspaperman's statement caused a momentary stir. Each person examined his or her neighbor.

Jack wrested the crowd's attention from Olson. "Thank you. Now Mr. and Mrs. Wakely, would you step up to the front door of Mr. Miller's office, and we'll get started?" Jack saw Buck in the back and waved him forward.

The doctor had arrived while Jack was speaking, and nodded to the undertaker, who had just shown up with a stretcher and two men. The undertaker addressed Jack. "If you are through with this young man, Marshal, I'll take him."

"If it's alright with the doc, it's fine with me." He left the two men to their gruesome job and stepped inside the office.

Buck followed him in. "What do you need me to do, Jack?"

"You heard what I said to the folks. Check each person for gunpowder smell or burns on their clothing. Also, look for blood splatters. Be thorough, but move as quickly as you can." He waved for the Wakelys to enter the office. He took the wife, and Buck the husband, who kept a close eye on Jack. When they had finished, Buck shook his head, and Jack nodded. "Ma'am, I apologize for the inconvenience, but I appreciate your cooperation. Thank you."

She smiled up at Jack. "Anything we can do to stop the killing in our town, we'll gladly do it." She shot her husband a pointed look. "Isn't that right, Mr. Wakely?"

"It sure is. Sorry I made such a fuss, Marshal."

"I understand your concern for your wife, Mr. Wakely, and I thank you."

The two exited the office, and Jack could hear Wakely speaking to the crowd. "Listen to me, everybody. There ain't nothin' to it. Buck and the Marshal were respectful and quick. Git on in here so you can git to bed."

Buck and Jack worked steadily for over an hour. Finally, the only ones standing at the door were the judge and the attorney, Miller. Jack waved them in, pointing the judge toward Buck.

The lawyer stopped. "You're checking us?"

Jack was tired. It had been a long day. He'd been in the saddle most of that time and had no desire to discuss anything with Miller.

His eyes hard, he stared at the man for a moment. "Get in here. It won't take but a minute."

The judge walked to Buck, who methodically examined his clothing and boots while Jack did the same to the attorney.

Judge Bell shot Jack an irritated glance. "I'll see you tomorrow."

Jack smiled. "Good night, Judge." He turned to Miller, thinking, *I at least should try to smooth this over a little bit so the judge won't have to listen to an earful.* "I appreciate the use of your office and apologize for the inconvenience, Mr. Miller. It was the closest office to the crowd and helped us keep them together. Had we tried to move everyone over to our office, we could have lost someone in the shuffle. See Buck with your bill. He'll make sure you are reimbursed."

The attorney said nothing, but slammed the door behind Buck, who was the last to leave his office. Light still streamed from the law office windows. Jack pulled his watch from his vest pocket. His thumb traveled over the emerald carved shape of the exploding grenade, which was embedded in the case of the watch, before he flipped it open. After checking the time, he snapped it shut and carefully dropped it back in his pocket. "Midnight. Walk with me back to Ma's place." The street was already deserted except for a couple of deputies in front of the marshal's office.

Jack adjusted his hat and stepped out. Buck fell in step with him. He glanced at his deputy. "I'm sure you figured out I accepted the judge's offer."

"And I'm glad you did. I know he was considering me, but I have no idea what to do with this bunch. I ain't never handled a bunch of men. I don't even know how much to pay Miller for the use of his office."

"Run it by Leon Nesbit. He'll show you. I've got news for you, Buck. You are going to be a marshal. Of course, you can turn it down, but would you really want to? You're the judge's first choice, and it won't be long before it happens. I accepted this job only temporarily. If you decide to accept it, you'll take over as marshal the first day of May."

13

Jack sat in a chair in front of the marshal's office. Buck was inside, going over the list of deputies, those on assignment and those available. The way the judge was coming up with assignments, it wouldn't be long before every marshal would be searching through the Indian Territory for desperadoes, and the available list would shrink to zero.

A wagon train had finished outfitting and was lined up, preparing to depart on its journey to Santa Fe. Jack felt good. This had been the best marshaling assignment he'd had since meeting Schofield. He had Buck doing most of the work, so it gave him time to be with the boys and Grace. They had begun packing and preparing for their departure to Texas. Matthew was excited about buying Ma's Bed and Eats. In fact, as far as Jack could tell, it appeared the chef had big plans for the boardinghouse. Mary had the wedding planned, assignments made, and it seemed she, like Jack, had time on her hands.

With less than three weeks remaining till the wedding, he was surprised he wasn't nervous. The only thing about the wedding that bothered him was the same thing that had bothered him in the beginning. The date was too far away.

He heard Buck cuss from inside the office. Jack grinned and thought, *I guess it's time to give him a hand.* Hiding behind Buck's wisecracking exterior was a born leader. Though he still complained, Buck was taking over with enthusiasm, and he didn't mind pitching in and working hard. He was becoming the type of leader almost any man would follow. They respected him, and most liked him. The paperwork was what gave him a major headache.

Jack rose and stepped through the door just in time to see his protégé pick up a sheet of paper, wad it into a ball, and hurl it at a trash can already surrounded with wadded paper balls.

"Hit a snag?"

Buck looked up, his face grim. "When are you leaving?"

Jack grinned. "On the first day of May. That's when Grace and I tie the knot and get on the riverboat for a relaxing and enjoyable run to Little Rock. The job will be all yours."

Buck grimaced. "That's less than three weeks. I think I'll quit. That's what I'll do. I'll head over to the judge and tell him I quit."

Jack laughed. "Go ahead. He'll string you up right next to one of those convicts he's hanging. Wouldn't that be a great ending to *Marshal* Buck Walker?"

Buck's grimace turned to a scowl. "You're enjoying this way too much."

Jack grabbed a chair and positioned it in front of the desk with the back facing Buck. He straddled it, pushed his hat to the back of his head, and crossed his arms over the top. "Listen to me, Buck. You're having the same problem every marshal in this country has: paperwork. It'll turn a man's hair gray faster than a gunfight.

"You need to set your mind at ease. You're doing a fine job, and anyway, the main thing is the way you handle your men. Now, I don't want your head getting so big your hat won't fit, but you've got the men on your side, and you aren't afraid to give orders. Boy, you've got this job treed. I could leave right now, and nobody would be the wiser." He pulled out his watch, opened it, checked the time, then snapped it shut. "Lunchtime. Grace had me shelling pecans last night. There'll be pecan pie on the table unless it's all gone by the time we get there."

Buck dropped the papers, jumped to his feet, and was past Jack in an instant. "You coming with me?"

Shaking his head, Jack stood and headed for the door behind his friend. "I'm guessing it isn't safe to get between you and pecan pie."

"You got it, Jack." Buck opened the door and turned back to Jack to speak when two shots blasted.

The bank, Jack thought. Through the windows and space separating the line of wagons, he saw three men dash from the bank with guns drawn. "Bank robbery!" He spun back to the gun rack and yanked two Winchester rifles from their stand, tossing one to Buck.

Both men dashed through the door and jerked their rifles to their shoulders, but they immediately pulled them down. "No shot. They're on the other side of the wagons. Get to the horses. I'm making a quick stop. Ask Pauly to saddle Smokey."

Men boiled out of the saloons and Ma's boardinghouse. Jack charged inside. Passing Grace, he yelled to her, "Bank's been robbed." In his room, he grabbed his rifle and tossed the one from the office on the bed. He also yanked his saddlebags from the back of a chair. They were always packed and ready for just such a situation. Racing through the kitchen, he stopped and jerked Grace into his arms, gave her a quick hug and kiss, released her, and was out the door, running for Pauly's stable. Buck raced by as he was entering the stable.

He yelled at the younger man to hold up, but with the excitement and the pounding hooves, there was no way he heard him. Jack uttered an oath under his breath. *I shouldn't have rushed out,* Jack thought. *It got Buck excited, and now all he'll be thinking about is catching them.* He saw Pauly had saddled

Smokey and thrown a bag of feed over the saddle horn. Jack took a second to fasten his saddlebags, swung into the saddle, and simultaneously waved to Pauly and yelled at Smokey. The grulla knew what the yell meant, and he launched through the barn door like his tail was on fire. The bank robbers had headed south.

I've got to get to Buck and slow him down, Jack thought. He gave Smokey his head and, dodging the people in the streets, raced from town. He leaned over Smokey's neck. "Come on, boy. Give it all you've got. If we don't catch that crazy lawman, the bank robbers might finish him."

He rounded a bend onto an almost due south straightaway. Ahead he could see Buck, and even as he spotted him, he saw the puff of smoke from the treeline ahead, and the younger man rolled from his saddle. Jack knew he couldn't hit anything at that distance and on the back of the speeding Smokey, but he looped his reins around the saddle horn, yanked his rifle from the scabbard and sent a barrage of bullets into the trees. He figured he must've come close, for there was no more firing from the trees. Reaching his friend's body, he yanked Smokey to a sliding stop.

Jack bailed out of the saddle and rushed to Buck's side. The deputy was limp as a dead rabbit, and blood was pouring from his head. Yanking his bandanna from around his neck, Jack wiped the wound channel, trying to see how deep the bullet penetrated. He breathed a sigh of relief. It had barely marked the bone, but the fast-moving piece of lead had left a three-inch crease along the top of Buck's head. Jack held the bandanna to the wound, picked up his friend, and carried him under a large walnut tree on the side of the road. After laying him in the grass, he looked around for their horses. Smokey was standing a short distance away, cropping grass, and Buck's horse had finally stopped near the gunman's treeline.

Jack divided his time between keeping watch in case the thieves should decide to finish the job, and holding the bandanna to Buck's head. "Pardner, you're gonna have to part your hair in the middle from now on."

Buck's eyes opened and jerked back and forth for a second before finally focusing on Jack. "I heard that, and it ain't funny. My head feels like someone slapped it with a blacksmith's hammer." He lifted a hand and wiped the blood from around his eyes. "Dang, that's a lot of blood. Am I dying?"

Jack shook his head. "A hardheaded cuss like you would need a heavier bullet than the one you were hit with to kill you. You've got a crease of about three inches along the top of your head. It looks like the bullet marked your skull, but that's it. I'm surprised it hurt a hardhead like you."

Buck's eyes narrowed. "It hurts alright, but not so much it'll keep me from gettin' after those bank robbers. They've marked me for life, and they're gonna pay for it."

Jack grinned. "Shoot, boy, the girls are gonna love it. A tough marshal like you. They'll be chasing you like bird dogs on a covey of quail. You may even beat me getting hitched."

"Very funny." He looked around. "Where's my hat?" Not seeing it close by, he pushed himself into a seated position. Remaining there for only a second, he dropped back to the ground. "Dizzy."

Jack heard hoofbeats approaching. "I don't doubt it after that lick your head took. Sounds like we're going to have company. Wait here."

From the ammunition loops on his gunbelt, Jack fed fresh rounds into his rifle. He had shot ten times into the treeline. His belt felt lighter from the missing cartridges. He watched the road and waited. The riders were coming from the direction of town. He relaxed when they rode into sight. Definitely not robbers. The doctor was one of the eight. There were three deputies and four other townsfolk besides the doc, one of which was the young teller, Casey Carter.

The doc lifted his bag from his saddle horn and dismounted.

He swung to the ground, went directly to Buck, and cleaned the wound.

Jack was glad to see Deputy Huck Porter was in the group. The man was an excellent tracker. No telling how long they'd be on the trail of the holdup men, but it wouldn't hurt to have a tracker with him.

Jack had learned Huck felt much like him when it came to cold weather. After spending several years in the Rocky Mountains, the man could no longer take the winters, so he'd headed south. His trek had brought him to Fort Smith, where Marshal Berry had talked him into joining the Marshal Service. That was five years ago. Every winter he threatened to quit and move farther south, but about the time he was reaching his limit, spring began.

"Huck, you'll be going with me. We'll leave just as soon as the doc gives us a report on Buck. By the way, was there anyone hurt in the robbery?"

Casey spoke up. "Mr. Gleason was the only one shot, Marshal. You'll have to ask Doc Freeman how he's doing."

Freeman, continuing to work on Buck, answered, "Gleason will be fine. The gunman almost missed. The shot clipped his arm. It cut a shallow channel through it, not even as deep as Buck's crease."

Buck raised up again, this time on his elbows, and used one arm to push the doc away. "Hold on, Jack. I'm going with you."

The doc dodged Buck's shove, and, placing his hand on the lawman's shoulder, pushed him gently back to the ground. "Not a chance. You're going back to my office. You've had a severe head injury, and I need to observe you to make further evaluations."

"Doc, let me up. I ain't gonna be staying behind. I've got a job to do."

Doc Freeman stood. "Fine. Let me give you a hand."

Buck extended his hand, and the doctor yanked him upright.

When he released Buck's hand, the lawman began swaying back and forth, and his arms waved like the wings of a drunk pelican.

"Alright, Doc. You made your point. Maybe I should sit down."

Jack and the doctor each grasped an arm and gently lowered him back to the ground. Once down, Buck laid his head back. "I could sure use my hat. This ground is hard."

The doctor had kneeled beside him and was watching Buck's eyes. "Look at this, Marshal. Watch his eyes."

Jack leaned over, placing a hand on each knee, and concentrated on Buck's eyes. They were jerking back and forth. While he watched, they slowed, stopped, and stared at him.

"Whatcha looking at, Jack?"

The doctor answered, "He's looking at why you won't be vertical for a while." He turned to the group of men still on horseback. "Casey, ride back to town and get a wagon from Pauly. Throw several blankets in it and get back here as quick as you can. Buck won't be walking or riding a horse for a few days."

Immediately Buck responded, "What do you mean, Doc? Are you deaf? I've got to get after those outlaws."

Jack kneeled by Buck and patted him on the shoulder. "It's not happening today, pardner. You heard the doc. Rest up, and let that head of yours heal. While you're getting better, you can catch up on that paperwork you were battling."

Buck's eyes narrowed, and his lips pursed. "I'm onto you, Jack. If I didn't know better, I'd say you had this done so you wouldn't have to do paperwork. Just let me get on my horse. I'll be fine. I don't need to be battling that blamed paperwork."

"Quit your bellyaching." Jack glanced at the doc. "How long you think it'll be before he's back on his feet?"

Doc Freeman shrugged. "That's something I can't say, Marshal. We don't know much about how the brain functions and responds to injuries. We've found that memory and balance can easily be affected after a hard fall or strike on the head, but we don't know why. Usually a patient recovers fairly quickly, but each person is different."

Huck had ridden a distance from the group, apparently searching for something. After leaning from his saddle, he galloped back, stepped from his horse, and walked to Buck's side. Bending over, he shoved Buck's shot and bloody hat under his head. "You're going to be needing a new hat, boss. But it'll work as a pillow."

Buck let out a long sigh. "Thanks, Huck. That feels mighty good." He pointed at Jack. "Keep this big galoot out of trouble, and catch those fellers who shot me. I'm almighty curious to know who's stupid enough to try to rob the bank in Fort Smith. I don't think there's any place that has more lawmen around."

"I'll sure do it, boss."

Jack glanced at the tracker. "You ready?"

"I was born ready, Marshal."

Jack nodded and looked down at Buck. "We're out of here. Tell Grace we may be gone for a while."

"I'll do it. Good luck to you."

"Luck to you." Jack headed for Smokey and swung into the saddle. Speaking to the other two deputies, Jack said, "Report to the judge what has happened, and let him know Huck and I are after the robbers."

The older of the two responded, "Will do, Marshal. Good hunting."

Jack swung Smokey toward the treeline where he had seen the smoke from the rifle blast, and Huck followed. Reaching the trees, Jack slowed, allowing the tracker to pass him and lead the way into the treeline. After entering the thicket, Huck pulled his horse to a stop and stepped down. Jack remained in the saddle. They didn't need two sets of boots obliterating whatever sign existed.

After a short time, Huck called softly, "Look at this, Marshal. I found where this feller was shooting from, and he was by himself. The rest of his compadres left him behind to do the dirty work."

Jack swung from Smokey, and Huck held out a .44 Henry case. "He only fired once. Your shootin' made him nervous. Looky here." He pointed at two fresh grazes cut into the tree's trunk above where the shooter had been kneeling. "Not close, but close enough to get him moving."

Jack took the case Huck was holding. The round was from a Henry or an 1866 Winchester, which fired the same caliber. It did little to narrow the field. There were a lot of men who used one or the other. "Tell me something we can use. Seems like every cowhand is carrying a Winchester or Henry these days."

Huck nodded. "Then how about this? Come on over here and take a look."

Jack moved carefully to Huck's side. The shooter had knelt against the right side of the hickory tree to brace his rifle against the thick trunk. He was kneeling on his left knee to brace the rifle's forearm against the tree. With his right foot acting as an additional brace, the heel was planted flat on the soft ground. The boot was outlined perfectly, and the heel left a clear impression of a five-point star inside a circle pressed into the dirt. Either the shooter's boots were newly soled or they were new boots, with the left, and probably the right, having the intact five-pointed star in the heel.

Huck let out a long squirt of tobacco. "Will that help?"

Jack laughed. "Yeah, Huck, all we have to do is bulldog the fella and check his boots."

Huck grinned. "I'll rope him. You throw him."

Jack started for Smokey. "Let's get out of here. I want to find these bank robbers before they have a chance to spend their money. Some of it's mine."

The two men stepped into the saddle and made their way along the trail. Slower this time. The results of Buck's pell-mell race were still fresh on their minds. The robbers weren't trying to conceal their tracks. They were riding their horses hard, but the animals were still maintaining long, confident strides. They'd have to be slowing soon unless they had fresh horses waiting for them.

Huck must have had the idea at the same time. He turned to Jack. "They've got horses waiting somewhere ahead."

Jack nodded. "You know of any place that would make a good relay station?"

The deputy started going over his thoughts aloud. "They'd need grass and water, at least. It'd also be nice to have a cache of food and supplies. Yep, about eight more miles, there be a stage station that has a stage passing through three times a week." He stopped talking for a moment. Jack could see Huck was deep in thought. It lasted for a few more seconds, then he turned to Jack. "Yes, sir, that could be it. The stage runs on Tuesday, Thursday, and Saturday. Today's Wednesday. There ain't no stage to interfere with them. That's where they're going." He grinned at Jack. "And I know a shortcut less than half a mile ahead."

"Let's go," Jack said. He bumped Smokey into a run, holding him back just enough to allow Huck to lead. *They could be waiting for us ahead,* Jack thought, bent over Smokey's neck, *but I doubt it. I think they're feeling confident since they saw Buck shot out of the saddle and me pull up.*

He and Huck raced down the road.

14

Approaching the almost invisible trail, Huck slowed to a walk and, spotting it, led them off the road.

Jack's countenance darkened at the thick foliage closing in on the narrow trail. "This trail will take us forever, as thick as it is."

"Just wait, boss. You'll see why I like it." Continuing until they had covered a little more than a hundred yards, the trail widened enough for two riders to ride side by side. Not only did it widen, but it was almost as open as the road they had just left. They urged their horses into a lope.

Jack glanced at Huck. "Will this really save us time?"

The older deputy nodded to the rhythm of his loping horse. "It sure will, Marshal. Unless those fellers can maintain the speed they were making coming out of town, we'll be there before they can switch horses and money."

"What's this trail used for?"

Huck laughed. "Rustlers." He shrugged. "And a few legitimate ranchers who know about it and need to move their cattle quickly without losing much fat. That's why it's so wide."

"How'd you find this trail? You're not from this part of the country, are you?"

The tracker shook his head. "Nope. I grew up in New York City, but I couldn't stand the city. I did a lot of reading about mountain men when I was growing up, and at fifteen, I ran away from home and traveled west. It was a tough life for a while, but I lived through it." Huck thought for a moment. "But you were asking me how I found out about the trail. I happened along one day at just the right time and actually saw a fella pushing sixteen cows from it onto the road. Seems he had borrowed them from a neighbor near the stage station. He's still servin' his time in the jail in Fort Smith."

Jack shook his head. "You came along at the right time."

"Yep, I sure did. Marshal, let's start slowing it up. We'll be breaking out of here in just a few minutes, and I want to look the country over and not just ride out into the open."

Jack slowed Smokey to a walk and dropped behind Huck. A few minutes later, the trail narrowed to an almost invisible deer run, with Jack ducking overhead limbs and brush dragging along his legs. Huck signaled, and they slowed their horses more and eased to the edge of the trees. Jack could see the stage station no more than two hundred yards ahead. They stood in the trees, watching. There was no movement around the station.

Too late, Jack thought. *Oh well, we're closer to them than we were. It's just a matter of time.* He was about to say something to Huck when a man led four saddled horses from the barn. Huck looked at Jack and grinned.

The man tied the horses to the hitching rail in front of the stage station and walked inside.

Jack leaned close to Huck. "We'll leave our horses here, then slip to the other side of the road and ease to the barn. I want to grab these robbers before they mount those horses."

"Good idea, boss."

Each man pulled his Winchester from the scabbard and

hurried across the road to the brush on the opposite side. Staying inside the treeline, the two lawmen slipped along the road until they had made it to the barn. Jack eased forward and peeked around the corner of the front wall. Still no movement.

"This way." He turned and trotted to the back of the barn, examined the interior through the open door, and slipped inside. Four lathered horses were further confirmation they had found their men. They continued through the barn until reaching the wide front door. They were less than thirty yards from the hitching rail where the horses were tied.

Loud voices, combined with laughter, reached them as the first man stepped through the open front door of the stage station. In a fit of laughter, the man bent over, grasped his knees, and gasped for breath. Jack couldn't make out every word, but enough was reaching him to cause his scalp to crawl. ". . . under their noses. All those marshals . . . knew exactly what he was talking about, and he didn't even want a cut." Jack heard clearly, "I think he's crazy, but it means more for us."

All four men were in the open, with a fifth man leaning against the door jamb, joining in the laughter. He wore a long apron and, as far as Jack could see, no gun. Jack turned to Huck. "Let's get them before they mount their horses."

Huck nodded his understanding, and the two marshals stepped out of the barn, rifles leveled at the men. Jack, his booming voice startling the robbers, demanded, "United States Marshals, boys. Drop your guns and live."

Three of the men froze, but the fourth didn't hesitate. He went for his Colt. Jack and Huck, shooting from the hip with their rifles, fired one shot each, immediately snapping the levers down and up, throwing out the fired cartridges, reloading the chambers, and cocking the hammers. The thump of the two bullets striking the man echoed across the hills, along with the muzzle blasts. The outlaw dropped to the ground, moaning and writhing in pain.

"I said drop your guns. If any of you make another move like that, we might be forced to fill you all full of lead."

Gunbelts dropped to the dirt, and the three remaining men reached for the clouds. "That's better," Jack said. "Now you boys move away from your horses and those guns. Move out into the open space there in front of the hitching rail."

The three men slowly stepped to the dusty area he had indicated.

Jack motioned to Huck, and they walked toward the robbers. "Alright, you three fellas lay facedown on the ground."

Each man knelt and then stretched out.

"Keep your hands high above your head."

All three followed Jack's directions. He glanced toward the empty doorway where the fifth man had stood, and raised his voice. "Alright, mister. You inside the stage station. Step outside here and join your friends."

There was no movement.

"Fella, I'm not saying this again. I don't know if you're involved with this bunch or not, and right now it doesn't make me any difference. If I have to come after you in that dark building, I'll shoot anything that moves, so you've got a choice. You can step out here and lie in the dirt where you'll be safe, or stay inside and die. It's up to you."

Seconds passed. Then, from inside the stage station, a voice yelled, "Don't shoot me. I'm coming out, and I ain't armed. My hands are up."

The man with the apron stepped through the open doorway and stopped, eyes glued on Jack.

"Anybody else in there?"

"No, Marshal, there ain't nobody else. These fellers were the only ones."

"You best not be lying to me, mister. I'm not long on patience right now."

Huck gave a short, barking laugh. "Let me tell you, boys. You may not know who you're dealing with. That there is Jack Sage. He's marshaled from New Mexico to Montana, and his favorite way to bring an outlaw in is over his saddle. He ain't never been known as being long on patience, so were I you, I wouldn't give him cause to pull that trigger."

The man in the apron's voice quivered. "I ain't lying, Marshal. I just keep the stage station operating. I ain't had nothing to do with these fellers. They wanted to leave some horses here, and I let 'em, that's all, and I'm all by myself here. I swear."

Listening to Huck, Jack battled to keep the grin from his face. *Not only is he an excellent tracker,* Jack thought, *but he's also full of horse apples. I'll give him credit, though. That little yarn should help keep these fellas in line.*

"Keep coming, mister. I want you facedown in the dirt, next to these other fellas." When the fifth man was stretched out on the ground, Jack pointed to the wounded man with his rifle. "Check him for weapons, but be careful. He's managed to roll around on his belly, and I can't see his right hand. When I see it, if it isn't empty, I'll put another one in his head."

The last statement was said more to the outlaw than Huck. Both men knew to be careful of a wounded man, especially the way he lay with his hand hidden under his body. Even though he had taken two .44-caliber slugs, he could still be dangerous, and if he came out with a weapon, Jack wouldn't hesitate to shoot him again. He eased forward with Huck, halting far enough back so he could cover all four men while he concentrated on the wounded man, who continued to moan, but also continued to hide his right hand under his belly.

Jack nodded to Huck. "Hold up just a second, Huck." Jack eased forward close enough to where he could poke the wounded man's head with the muzzle of the rifle. He shoved it forward until it rested on the top of the man's head. "Mister, my friend's gonna roll you over. If you've got a gun under there, I'd recommend you leave it lying in the dirt, or you're gonna get the muzzle of my Winchester mighty bloody."

He nodded to Huck, who, standing on the left side of the wounded man, squatted, getting as low as he could, and grasped his right shoulder. Slowly, he lifted the man toward him and rolled him until he dropped on his back. There, where he had been lying, was a double-barreled .44-caliber derringer. Huck reached across the man and picked up the wicked-looking little two-barreled weapon and lowered the hammer, sliding the tiny weapon behind his belt. The man's eyes tracked his movements.

"Leaving that derringer in the dirt was a mighty smart move, mister." Jack had stepped back so he could continue to easily cover the other four men. "Although you wouldn't be stretched out on the ground, bleeding to death, if you hadn't made a mighty dumb move."

Without moving his head, the outlaw moved his eyes up so that he could watch Jack. "I'm fast, mister." He coughed, wincing with pain, before continuing, "I might have got you."

Jack shook his head. "Only in your dreams, fella. Even I wouldn't try to beat a drawn gun unless I knew I was going to die if I didn't. You had no such worry. You boys didn't kill anyone. The worst that will happen to your friends here is they'll go to jail for a few years. Then they'll get out and be none the worse for wear, unlike you. You'll be dead shortly."

Huck broke in, kicking the wounded man's boots. "Here he is, Jack. This is the feller who shot Buck. He's got the star on his boot heels." Huck looked up and grinned at Jack. "How's that for a mighty fine clue?"

A sideways grin slipped across Jack's face. "That was a good clue, Huck. Exactly what I'd expect from a master tracker."

Huck's grin widened, but he said nothing, just kicked one of the bushwhacker's boots again.

Jack grew serious again, speaking to the group of outlaws. "Who's the head honcho here?"

One of the other men spoke. "That'd be me, Marshal."

"What about you, Mr. Station Manager? Are you sure you're not involved with this bunch?"

The man shook his head in the dirt. "No, sir. I told you the truth. They just came by a couple of nights ago and asked if they could keep some horses here. That's all. I swear, Marshal."

Jack glanced at his deputy. "Huck, go get the greener I suspect is behind this fella's bar and anything else he might have that could affect our health."

The deputy disappeared inside the building. He was back a few minutes later with an additional Colt Peacemaker in his belt and a short-barreled 12-gauge shotgun in his hand. "That's all I could find, Jack. The place looks like a stage station, although a dirty one. That feller could be telling you the truth."

Jack swung the barrel of his Winchester to cover the station manager. "My deputy seems to think you might be an honest man, but I haven't decided yet. I'm thinking, if you're so honest, why were you laughing so hard at these fellas' jokes about robbing the bank in Fort Smith?"

"Can I get up?"

"Carefully."

One of the outlaws spoke, causing dust to puff away from his mouth. "What about us, Marshal? It's mighty dirty down here."

"I don't think a little dirt will hurt you fellas at all. Stay there."

The wounded man moaned. "Marshal, that sun's mighty hot. Can I get inside?"

"Can you walk?"

The man's voice was weaker. "Don't reckon I can, Marshal."

Jack glanced at the station manager. "Where's your helper?"

"He quit a couple of days ago. I've got to get a new one, but I'm by myself right now."

Jack pointed his Winchester at the wounded man. "Why don't you grab him under his arms and drag him inside. You can stretch him out on one of your tables, and see if there's anything you can do for him. You do have tables in there, don't you?"

"We do, Marshal. I might need a hand getting him on the table."

Jack thought for a second. *I don't want to split these fellas up so that only one of us is watching each group.* He shot a glance at Huck. "Give these fellas a good search, boots, belts, everywhere."

Huck went to work, while the wounded man's moans grew quieter. Knives, derringers and pocket pistols came out of boots, backs of shirts between shoulder blades, and under shirt fronts. He tossed the weapons in a pile, well away from the outlaws. "Finished, Jack."

"Alright, boys, stand up nice and slow."

The three men stood, and Jack assessed each man. Deciding, he waved the youngest of the bunch toward the wounded man, whose moans had stopped. "You. Give the station manager a hand and move your friend onto a table inside.

"Huck, lead them in, and keep them covered. If either makes a move toward you, shoot him. It'll make an easier job of getting them back to Fort Smith."

"Glad to, boss. I have little patience with this kind. Since they shot Buck, taking them back alive doesn't rank real high on my importance scale."

Jack nodded to the younger outlaw. "Alright, young fella, grab hold of your friend's feet and help get him inside."

The young man stepped to his partner's feet and waited until the manager lifted him by the shoulders. The wounded man's head lolled back, and his mouth pulled open.

Jack motioned to Huck. "Check him. I think he's dead."

Huck motioned the men to step away, kneeled, and pulled back first one eyelid and then the other. Shaking his head, he stood. "Boss, he's gone."

"Take him to the barn, then come right back. We'll wait."

Jack eyed the remaining pair. "Alright, boys, let's start with names, and we'll begin with you, big fellow."

The man, uneasy under Jack's gaze, first looked at the remaining man, then back at Jack. "You want my name, Marshal?"

"That's what I said. Spit it out."

"It's Zeke, Marshal. That's short for Ezekiel. My ma named me for one of them prophets in the good book."

"What's your last name, Zeke?"

"Anderson, Marshal." He tossed a thumb toward the man standing close by. "This here is my brother, Jed. That's short for Jedediah. It's from the Bible, too. Ma named all of her kids from the Bible." Nodding his head, Zeke looked at his brother. "Ain't that right, Jed?"

He sounds just like Art Livingston's boys, Jack thought.

The young fella, Huck, and the station manager returned from the barn. Jack motioned for the two men to fall in next to Zeke.

Zeke pointed at his partner. "That youngster is Vern Lee. Cole thought he was fast, but Vern is plenty quick, too." He grinned at Vern. "Ain't that right, Vern, boy?"

Jack reasoned he had found a fount of information in Zeke, so he continued, "What's Cole's last name, Zeke?"

"Yes, sir, he'd be Cole Baker, the gunfighter. Can you believe he'd ride with us? He's the one who found out about the bank safe. Why, we never would've robbed that bank except Cole got the combination to the safe." He turned again to his brother. "Ain't that right, Jed? Why, you said, even then, that was about the most dangerous bank in the world to rob, what with all them marshals around. You said that, didn't you, Jed?" His brother, Jed, nodded, but Zeke went on. "Yes, sir, I remember you telling us if we had to kill a marshal or two for that much money, it'd be worth it. We'd just run down to South America and live like kings."

"Shut up, Zeke," Jed said, his eyes showing a combination of anger and fear as his head jerked back to Jack. "Marshal, my brother's slow. He don't rightly remember everything exactly the way it happened."

Jack focused cold gray eyes on the outlaw. "I tend to think he's remembering exactly what happened, and Jed, you shut up. I don't want to hear another word out of your mouth." He looked back at Zeke. "Did Cole tell you who gave him the combination?"

Zeke, a hurt expression on his wide face, had been looking at his brother. When Jack asked, the big man's blue eyes turned back to him. "No, he sure didn't. Why, he said this feller slipped up behind him in the dark. He even pulled a gun on Cole. Cole said he heard the hammer being pulled back. After telling him not to turn around, the man told him there was a bunch of money in the bank and gave him the combination. You ain't gonna believe this, but he didn't even want a share." A look of wonder settled on Zeke's face, and he stared at Jack, shaking his head.

"So you didn't find out who gave Cole the bank information?"

"Nope, that was all he knew."

Continuing with the questioning, Jack asked, "You're telling me your brother is the boss?"

Now Zeke began nodding enthusiastically. "He sure is, and he's mighty smart. When we robbed that stage down close to Little Rock, why, he found out they were carrying gold, figured out where to stop it, and got us out of there with no one getting shot. That's pretty smart, ain't it, Marshal?"

"It sure is, Zeke. That's really smart." He gave Jed a warning glance, knowing the man was going crazy with fear over what his brother might say next.

The station manager raised his hand. "Marshal, since I'm by myself here, I've got a lot to do before the stage comes in tomorrow. If you ain't gonna arrest me, you mind if I get busy?"

Jack gave the man a long look. He seemed honest, but Jack

thought, *I've been fooled by honest-looking people before.* He glanced at Huck, who must've been reading his mind, for the deputy gave him a nod and a shrug. The thought slipped through his mind, *My feelings exactly. This fella was here with these outlaws and from what we saw was getting along mighty well, but what can you really tell about facial expressions from a distance?* "What's your name, mister?"

"Name's Wilbur Morgan, Marshal. I been with this here stage company for nearly ten years. I ain't never stole a thing, not even a bucket of oats. The company trusts me with this station. If you let me go, you won't regret your decision."

The speech did it for Jack. Actually, the ten-year bit sold him. No company would keep a man for ten years who hadn't showed his honesty, not that an honest man couldn't turn bad. Jack made his decision. "Mr. Morgan, you get me piggin' strings to tie these fellas up, and you're free to get back to your work."

After Morgan hurried inside his stage station, Jack motioned toward the prisoners. "First thing, Huck, we need to do is get these fellas secured." The sound of running feet behind him caused him to stop. He started to turn and heard Huck yell, "Look out!"

Even as Jack spun to bring his Winchester to bear, Huck was thrown back like he'd been kicked in the chest by a mule, and the crash of a Spencer filled the yard. Morgan's wide eyes glared at him from the corner of the house. Jack dove to the side, thinking, *I should never have trusted you, Morgan. I knew there was something wrong about you, and now I've killed Huck.*

He fired an instant before Morgan and could see the man's wide-eyed stare disappear in a fog of blood. Jack hit the ground while working the lever of his Winchester and rolled toward the three outlaws behind him. The last thing he remembered was the sight of a boot coming straight for his head.

15

Darkness surrounded him. An owl hooted nearby, and something scraped bark from high in a tree. There were no man sounds. He reached a hand to his face, and it came away wet and sticky, blood. *I have to be able to see,* he thought. Bringing both hands to his face, he carefully ran his fingers over the cut and torn skin. He felt the skin of his forehead push back like a flap on an army holster. Reaching up to his hairline, he pressed the loose flap tight as best he could and smoothed it against the surface. Blood began to flow again. He couldn't sew it because he couldn't see.

Number one priority was his vision. His fingers moved to his right eye. It was swollen closed. The left didn't feel as large, but like the right, it was sealed tight with dried blood. He had to find water, but how if he couldn't see? If he started crawling, he could just as easily be crawling away from the water as to it.

His faculties were returning. The weight of his sixguns on his hips was gone. *Of course they took our weapons*, he thought. Jack took a deep breath, and a sharp pain filled the right side of his chest. *At least one broken rib, probably more*. With the sharp pain came the harsh memory of Huck thrown back from the bullet strike of the Spencer. The memory brought a moment of self-recrimination. *I'm the reason Huck is dead. I should never have let Morgan out of my sight. Follow my gut. That's always been rule number one, and I didn't, and now Huck pays for my mistake.* He began a deep breath again, a precursor to another sigh, and the pain from the broken ribs stabbed through his chest. *Stop it,* he thought. *Enough with the self-pity. It's your fault. Live with it. Your goal right now is to get your eyes open. You need water.*

Something large moved near Jack, something very large. He felt as much as heard the presence. Then it blew in his face. He reached out and felt the horse's head. Grabbing the bridle, Jack spoke softly. "Easy, boy." He pulled his legs under him. His right hip hurt like the blazes. A touch of humor returned in his depth of pain when he thought, *Great, they had to kick my old beat-up leg.* With the help of the horse, Jack pulled himself to his feet. "Smokey? Is that you, boy?"

He held the bridle in his left hand and slowly slid his right along Smokey's neck to his front shoulder and touched the saddle. His hand went for the saddle horn, around which hung the leather strap he was hoping for, his canteen. Jack felt a flash of jubilance. Holding tight to the horn, he pulled the canteen to his mouth and took several long swigs. Finally, he forced himself to stop. *That's just what I need to do,* he thought, *drink the water that's needed to clean my eyes.*

Jack pulled the bandanna from around his neck and soaked one corner of it with water. It took only a few minutes before his left eyelid was clean of the dried blood. It opened enough for him to see it was nighttime. His vision wasn't clear, but he could see.

In the moon's light, Huck's lifeless body lay on the dry ground in front of the stage stop. He leaned on Smokey and stared at the deputy, replaying the sudden change in their destiny. It had all been going to plan until it wasn't.

Now with some semblance of his vision back, he moved to his saddlebags, opened one side, and pulled out one of his spare .44-

Caliber Smith & Wessons. He checked the loads and dropped it into the empty holster on his right side. The outlaws had taken all of their weapons, but evidently, they hadn't looked for the horses. *It makes sense,* Jack thought. *They wanted to get far away from this gruesome scene as quickly as possible. That's probably why they didn't put a bullet in me, or they figured I'd die from the beating. I'll make a point of asking them.*

He went to work on cleaning his right eye. This eye was much worse than his left. It was swollen closed and then sealed with thick, caked blood. He worked on it until he had it clean, but it still wouldn't open. *Give it time,* he thought. Jack led Smokey to the water, but the horse wasn't interested. There was feed in the barn, and the barn was open, so the big grulla had probably had all he wanted to eat and drink. Hopefully not too much, Jack thought. He led Smokey to the hitching rail and tied him. Those slight efforts used all of his energy, and he dropped into one of the chairs Morgan had set outside against the station wall. He still held the canteen, so he took a couple more swigs, shoved in the stopper, and leaned his head against the plank wall.

The rattle and squeak of the stage woke him. His neck was stiff and so sore he could hardly move it. His face, and especially his forehead, was a pincushion of pain. He opened his eyes to faint light, his left eye opened normally, and his right opened a crack. The left eye had cleared, but through his right, he saw everything in a red haze. The stage wheeled around the tall red oak in the yard and pulled to a stop, feet from Huck's body.

Jack knew the stage driver, Birch Graham. Like most, his nickname was Whip. Birch flipped the reins of the six horses around the brake handle and jumped to the ground. He ran around the back of the coach, stopping at Huck's body, which was beginning to swell.

The fella riding shotgun dropped and stepped to his side. "Whip, I never thought there was a bullet what would take old Huck."

Whip shook his head and stepped to Jack. "Marshal Sage, you're looking mighty bad. You shot anywhere?"

Jack shook his head carefully. His neck was so stove up he could hardly move it. "No. For some reason, they didn't shoot me. I think after they knocked me out and whaled the tar out of me, they wanted to get out of here as quickly as they could." He pointed to the treeline where he and Huck had tied their horses. "Huck's horse may still be tied in there. He hasn't had water since yesterday afternoon. Can one of you fellas untie him and get him to the trough? I'm sure Huck would be much obliged."

Whip motioned to the shotgun. "Lyman, go check on him."

Without a word, Lyman, holding his shotgun in his left hand, trotted toward the treeline.

Whip leaned down and examined Jack's face. "You're pretty messed up, Marshal. What'd they do to you? Looks like a spur was dragged across your cheek, and the skin on yore forehead is torn back mighty bad."

Whip raised up and looked around, as if seeing the stage station for the first time. "Where's Morgan? He's supposed to have me a team ready to go, and some food thrown together for these folks. Though he ain't much of a cook."

Jack nodded at Huck. "Morgan killed him."

Whip looked at Jack like he was crazy. "Wilbur? You mean Wilbur Morgan? Why, that feller's the nicest son of a gun I've ever seen."

Jack could see the disbelief on the stage driver's face. He dipped his head toward the corner of the building. "He stepped from around that corner with a Spencer, and without a word of warning, he blasted Huck."

Whip shook his head. "That's hard to believe about Wilbur, Marshal."

"Then go take a look at him, what's left. His corpse is stretched out behind that wall."

Whip spun and headed for the corner of the building as two

men from the stage stopped and stared at Huck and then Jack. Behind them, a young woman strode forward and pushed between them. "Get out of my way!" She paused long enough to assess Huck and then stepped up to Jack. "Driver, stop staring at that dead man and help me with the living. Can't you see this man needs doctoring? Find a station hand, or you go inside and start heating water." She looked at one of the men she had just pushed past. "Don't just stand there, get me one of those chairs, and get that body covered."

Hurrying from Morgan's body, Whip rushed past Jack, shaking his head and muttering in disbelief.

She called to him as he disappeared into the station, "You can also get a pot of coffee started. This man needs a stimulant, and coffee will help."

The passenger she had been addressing had a chair for her before she stopped talking. She gave him a radiant smile. "Thank you, sir. Now if you would, bring that other chair over here so I can place my bag on it." The second man leaped to comply. A moment later, with her bag resting on a chair next to her, she opened it and pulled out a stethoscope. Placing the earpieces in her dainty ears and grasping the round portion in her small hand, she pressed it against Jack's chest.

Jack grinned, though the movement brought pain to his face. "It's still beating, ma'am."

"Shh." She continued listening. Then moved it to another spot on his chest. "Take a deep breath."

Jack managed a quarter breath, and his inhalation jerked to a stop from the pain in his ribs.

"Broken ribs," she said to herself. She finished with his chest by listening to the opposite side. "This time, Marshal, inhale only as much as you can without causing yourself pain. Lean forward."

Jack did as he was told and took two more deeper than normal breaths.

"Your heart and lungs are fine."

She shot an impatient look at the door and took a deep breath. The men watched her, for she was a very attractive woman, and each time she breathed deeply, she swelled her modest dress quite nicely.

Jack stopped her. "Ma'am, he likes to be called Whip. That's the nickname for stage drivers."

She nodded. "Thank you, Marshal." After taking another deep breath, she called again. This time the sharp edge was gone from her voice. "Mr. Whip, how is the water coming?"

Whip's yell could've been heard five miles away. "Looks like it'll be boiling in just a minute, ma'am."

"And the coffee? I could also use a cup. I imagine these gentlemen could, too."

"Yes, ma'am. It'll be ready in just a minute, and those *gentlemen* can march themselves in here if they want a cup."

"Thank you. Could you also bring me a couple of clean towels, please?"

While the conversation was going, Jack watched the shotgun rider, Lyman, bring Huck's horse to the water trough in front of the barn. The horse shoved its muzzle into the water and drank deeply until Lyman pulled the animal's head from the water.

". . . your face."

With a blank look, Jack brought his eyes back to the woman. "Ma'am?"

"Marshal, your face is cut and bruised very badly." She gently pressed the flap of skin on his forehead. "I'm going to have to do a bit of sewing, and it will be quite painful. Laudanum will help. I suggest you let me mix some for you before we begin."

"No, ma'am, I won't be drinking any laudanum, but I could sure use a cup of coffee."

"It is going to hurt, Marshal." She stopped. "I'm Sue Bryson. What is your name, Marshal?"

"Ma'am, it is Jack Sage. Are you a doctor?"

"Call me Sue, and if you don't mind, I shall call you Jack, and no, I am not a doctor, but I am a nurse, and I have sewn many a man's wounds."

Whip came out with two cups in one hand and the bail of a half-full pot of steaming water in the other. One passenger followed with several stained but clean dish towels. The man turned and went back inside, returning with another chair, on which he placed the towels.

Sue smiled at both men. "Thank you, gentlemen." She took a sip of coffee, returned her cup to the chair, and lifted a small packet from her case. Opening it, she exposed several needles. She looked at his wound again and selected a needle. After stringing it with what looked like a heavy thread, she turned to Jack. "Are you ready?"

Jack was feeling some better. The broken ribs still hurt, but he could manage with those, and the facial pain had dissipated. Looking at the needle, he figured the pain level was about to increase. "Yes, ma'am."

She leaned forward, stopped, and slid her chair closer, positioning herself next to Jack. He could smell the dying fragrance of a flowery perfume mixed with the perspiration of long travel. Unconsciously, his nostrils flared imperceptibly.

"I'm sorry if my odor is offensive, Jack. Traveling on a stage for several days does not provide many opportunities to clean one's self."

Jack started to shake his head, but at that instant, Sue shoved the point of the needle through his torn flap of skin near the scalp, creating a small but intense point of pain. He showed nothing. "No, ma'am, you don't smell bad at all. In fact, you smell nice."

She continued to sew. He could feel the stitches close together. There would be many more stitches than he had figured. Though the morning was cool, beads of sweat appeared along Jack's hairline. Sue worked swiftly. Jack figured she had been a military nurse somewhere and must be traveling to join someone out west.

Jack drank his coffee as she worked. He watched the concentration on her face. "Where are you headed?"

"To Fort Smith." She worked steadily as she talked. "Doc Freeman and his wife are good friends, and he sent me an offer of employment." One side of her mouth lifted in a wry smile. "He says there's a booming business there."

Jack laughed. "Booming is right."

He heard pots, pans, and dishes rattling inside. Lyman had taken care of Huck's horse and was now inside with Whip, trying to put something together for the passengers' breakfast while Sue continued working on Jack. He could hear Whip talking. "We got to get going as soon as we can. We're already way behind schedule. Plus, we'll have Huck and Marshal Sage on board. That's more weight."

Jack raised his voice. "You don't have to worry about me. I'm not going with you."

Whip stepped out the door. "What do you mean, Jack? You need to get to the doctor." He glanced at Sue. "No offense meant, ma'am."

"You're right. What I'm doing is only temporary."

It was all Jack could do to keep from grimacing when she pulled the thread tight. He could see her hands making quick movements, then with her free hand, she reached into her bag, pulled out a pair of scissors, and cut the thread, creating an audible snip.

"The torn skin on your forehead is sewn in place, Jack. But Mr. Whip is right. You need to see the doctor. He has medicines that are much more suitable for your wounds than mine. The ones I'm using are for general use."

"That's nice, ma'am, but I'm not going back to Fort Smith. There's three men out there who are responsible for the death of a United States Deputy Marshal, and I aim to bring them to justice."

She had wet a towel and was cleaning the other wounds on his face, but she stopped and sat back, staring at him. "Jack, are you crazy? That flap of skin needs a doctor's attention. Even with the best of care, it could fail to adhere to your forehead and will have to be removed surgically. If it doesn't receive proper care, you could die."

She leaned forward and resumed cleaning Jack's face.

"Ma'am, we all die. Those men have to be brought to justice." He looked around. "And frankly, the only one I see around here wearing a badge is me."

Her lips pursed. She threw the cloth with which she had been cleaning Jack's face into the bucket. "You men are so unreasonable. Don't you understand the danger of what you are doing? I am serious, Marshal Sage. You could die."

Jack nodded at Huck's covered body. "Yes, ma'am. I think I'm aware of that possibility."

He started to stand, but her small hand shot out, grabbed his sleeve, and gently pulled him back down. "Please. Wait. At least let me send you on your way with as much chance as possible. Let me finish cleaning your face."

Jack eased back into the chair. He had to admit his face felt better. Even his forehead wasn't burning as badly as it had.

"Besides the flap of skin on your forehead, you have one, two, three, four punctures in your right cheek. They should heal fine." She leaned in close and stared into first his right eye and then his left. "Your right eye may take a few days to recover from the abuse it has taken. You're very lucky his spur did not reach your eye. As far as I can tell, it should heal without any loss of sight. In fact, you should have near perfect vision in your left eye right now."

Jack looked around the yard. His left eye seemed to work fine. Suddenly, he thought about Smokey for the first time since the stage arrived. *I can't believe I haven't gotten the saddle off and let him roll and rest.* He raised his voice. "Lyman?"

The shotgun rider stepped outside. "Yes, sir, Marshal. What can I do for you?"

"Did you see the grulla in the barn?"

"I surely did. I unsaddled him and put out corn for him along with the hay."

Relief flooded Jack. Smokey had been there for him whenever he had called on the big horse. "Thanks, I appreciate you doing that."

"Why sure, Marshal. Didn't figger you'd be up to it for a while."

Jack nodded and stood. He expected to be dizzy and unbalanced, but he actually felt pretty good, with a few exceptions.

Sue stood facing him. "We're not finished, Marshal."

Jack's forehead hurt when he frowned. "Ma'am, I don't understand."

"Your ribs."

"Oh. I reckon they'll just have to heal on their own."

"Yes, they will, but we can give them a little help." She turned toward the station door. "Mr. Whip, would you mind getting my suitcase for me, please?"

Whip stepped outside. "Ma'am, we need to be leaving, not unpacking the top of the coach."

Her demanding voice changed into a sweet, pleading tone. "Oh, I am so sorry, but I need something out of my suitcase to take care of the marshal. If you could help, I would so appreciate it."

Whip turned toward the stagecoach. His grumbling was indistinct except for the word women mentioned more than once. She turned and gave Jack a conspiratorial smile. He shook his head, carefully.

She thanked the stage driver profusely, laid her suitcase on the ground, opened it, and took out a voluminous white petticoat.

After removing it, she picked up her scissors and began cutting it in a wide, continuous strip. Several times she stopped and measured Jack with her eyes and began again. Finished, she laid the bundle of cut petticoat on a chair and turned to Jack. "Take off your shirt and pull down your long johns top."

Jack had figured out what she had in mind, and since he was going to be riding a horse with broken ribs, he was more than willing to go along with her idea. He removed his shirt and lowered his long johns. At forty-one, his flat stomach, muscular chest, and thick biceps were still impressive.

Sue eyed him for a moment with her eyebrows raised. "My, my, you are quite a sight. Hold your hands as high as you can."

16

Cleaned and bandaged, Jack watched the stage pull out, Huck's body wrapped and lying on top. Huck's horse would remain at the stage station until Jack or another marshal came through, headed for Fort Smith.

Jack had finished the meal Whip prepared, and it wasn't half bad. With food in his stomach, he was feeling better and was pleased his right eye was showing improvement. Lyman had saddled Smokey for him, and Whip's Winchester was riding in his scabbard. He thought he was going to have to fight the stage driver to pay him for the rifle, but he finally accepted.

The nurse, Sue Bryson, had warned him one last time about his travels. The warning included his face and the possibility of a broken rib puncturing his lung from the constant jarring on horseback. When he quietly insisted he was going after the outlaws, she shook her head and wished him good luck.

Lyman had stayed to man the station until a new station manager was sent out. He wasn't happy about it. He liked riding shotgun and having his free time when he wasn't on a run. Here, he would work all the time. He sat next to Jack, watching the stage disappear.

"She was quite a woman, wasn't she, Marshal?"

"Yes, she was. I don't think there'll be too many men putting anything over on her."

Lyman laughed. "No, sir. I'm sayin' you're right. Whatever man persuades her to hitch up with him is going to have his hands full. Yessiree. He surely is."

Jack began a grin, but halted at the pain. After the stage disappeared, he stood and looked down at Lyman. "I best be on my way. You going to be alright?"

Lyman also stood. "I surely am, Marshal." He patted the shotgun he held. "I've got ole meat-in-the-pot here. I'll be just fine. How about you?"

Jack nodded to the man and started for Smokey. "Yep. I'll be better on the trail than I would be sitting around here growing moss."

"I know what you mean, Marshal. Reckon I'll be sittin' around trying to figure out what got into Morgan. I guess money can fog a man's brain." He spit and shook his head. "I hope they get me out of here as fast as they can."

Jack grasped the saddle horn, slid his left foot into the stirrup, and swung his right leg up and over, finding the other stirrup with the toe of his boot. He thought, *I'm glad Sue sacrificed her petticoat. I don't know how I would have managed without this wrapping. It makes a real difference with this rib.*

He settled in the saddle and reached for his borrowed watch. The outlaws had taken his. This was the second time the watch had been stolen. With the emerald set in the cover, it was a tempting target for any thief. *They just better take care of it,* he thought. *I'd be sorely tempted to kill any man who damaged it from carelessness or spite.*

The watch he was currently using was Huck's. He'd return it to his friend's belongings when he returned to Fort Smith. It showed the time was nine in the morning. He shook his head at the thought. *All the work Sue did on me, and it's only nine o'clock.*

That's good. I don't think Jed and his gang expect anyone to be on their trail today, and definitely not this early.

He knew he was going to miss Huck's tracking skills. Though Jack was an excellent tracker, he wasn't the quality tracker Huck had been. His mind tried to drift to the shooting, but he pushed it back into a corner of his mind. He would save it for later.

He bumped Smokey into a lope. Each footfall sent pain through his chest, but he handled it. He could rest later. He hadn't traveled far down the road when it turned east. A trail sliced off to the south. The outlaws' tracks were obvious where they had turned along the trace.

"Boy," Jack said to Smokey, "looks like these fellas have a destination in mind. Hope you feel like staying on their trail. I figure Grace is going to be a little upset if I don't make the wedding date. Hopefully, this ugly mug of mine won't scare her off."

Jack turned the big grulla onto the trail. Looking ahead, the trail was straight like a thin line darkening in the distance, under tall pines, sumac, willow, and oak.

~

EIGHT DAYS LATER, an exhausted, bearded, swollen, bruised, and sore Jack Sage rode an equally tired Smokey into the thriving metropolis of Texarkana, Arkansas. Jack had been amazed at the number of creeks between Fort Smith and Texarkana. He felt like he and Smokey had spent as much time in the water as on the trail.

Pointing Smokey toward the first livery he came to, the grulla smelled water and headed for the trough. Reaching it, Jack swung down, holding to the saddle horn for a few seconds while he exercised his right leg. The outlaws' kicks to his injured right leg hadn't improved its use. The leg was stiff and painful.

"Howdy, mister," a call came from inside the barn. A tall,

skinny, old man with a well-trimmed mustache and a distinct limp stepped from the stable and, head down, made his way to Jack. Reaching him, he looked into Jack's face, and his blue eyes opened wide. "Glory be, feller. You been run over by a stampede?"

Jack grinned, thankful his face would at last allow him to spread his lips without pain. "It appears so, doesn't it?"

The liveryman's attention finally left Jack's face to see the star on his chest. "Marshal, well, sir. You needing to see a doctor? We got a good one in town, a couple, in fact. Since the railroad come, we're growing hand over fist. By the by, you can call me Micah."

Jack shook his head. "No doc now, Micah. The name's Jack Sage. First, I'd like you to take care of my horse. The poor old fella has had a rough week. He needs grain, corn or oats, or both, and a good rubdown."

"Looks like he might like a washing first." Micah picked off several chunks of mud from Smokey's right hind leg.

"That too, but maybe a feedbag while he gets washed. He's mighty hungry."

"I can sure do that for him. He looks like a fine horse, only just about worn to a frazzle." With a gray eyebrow pulled high, he surveyed Jack. "I reckon he ain't the onliest one."

Jack nodded. "Micah, I'm looking for three men. They are probably big spenders, although I imagine their clothes would look about as bad as mine."

Micah was nodding his head. "Yes, sir. They rode into town maybe four hours ago. They was asking about a train to Galveston. I told them ain't nothing running to Galveston yet. They'd have to go to Dallas first. I'll tell you, Mr. Marshal, to my way of thinkin', most folks going to Galveston are planning on leaving the country." He shot a long stream of tobacco that struck a motionless rat. Most of the juice struck the little rodent directly in his ear. He gave his head a violent shake and scurried into the barn. Micah frowned and muttered, "Danged rats, cats are falling down on their jobs."

"You have any idea when the next train leaves for Dallas?"

"They asked me the same question, and I told them I ran a stable, not a train station. The boss seemed to get a little riled at my answer, but the big fella calmed him down. They wanted to sell me their horses. They had some excellent stock, but those animals' ribs were sticking out like they'd never seen an ounce of fat. Looked like they'd put in some hard riding for several days."

"They robbed the bank in Fort Smith."

"Aha, yep, that explains it. I offered those boys a third of what their horses were worth, and they took it, no haggling, no questions asked, no complaining. Sold me the whole she-bang, saddles and all, and then the crazy fools gave me a twenty-dollar tip." He shook his head. "These younger folks are just plain stupid."

"So you don't know when the next train to Dallas leaves?"

Micah gave Jack a snaggletoothed grin. "Course I do, Marshal. I got a schedule right inside my office. It has all the departures and arrivals. I aim to help my customers."

"You didn't help them."

"I didn't like 'em, not one bit."

Jack laughed. "You're an excellent judge of character, Micah. Not only did they rob the bank of honest folks' money, but they killed a United States Marshal."

Smokey had stopped drinking, so Micah took the horse's reins and started toward the barn, motioning for Jack to follow. "By the by, Marshal. The Dallas train ain't leaving till six in the morning, and there ain't another eastbound train afore then."

Jack gave a chuckle. "So I guess you like me."

With a glint in his clear blue eyes, Micah glanced at Jack. "The jury's still out on you, exceptin' your taking care of your horse. That rates mighty high in my book."

"Thank you, Micah. Can you tell me if they mentioned where they might go?"

"Those boys kept talking about being mighty thirsty and in need of female companionship. I told them there were two places that catered to both of their needs, the Belmont House and the Silver Dollar. One of 'em, right loud, said, 'The Silver Dollar 'cause we've got plenty of those.' The others thought that was mighty funny, and they all laughed like crazy. Them fellers took off right after that. They left everything, including their bedrolls, but they took their saddlebags. All three bags were stuffed with something."

Jack thought, *Money.* "Is there a sheriff or town marshal in Texarkana?"

"Yes, sir, we got both, and the sheriff's in town. I know because he keeps his and the county's riding stock with me. The sheriff's also got the best jail, stronger, but they're both good men."

"Where do I find their offices?"

"Just keep heading on down the street. The sheriff's is first. A little farther and you'll find the marshal. They're both on this side, the Arkansas side. You might have noticed the name of the street is State Street. On the east side is Arkansas, and on the right is Texas. Ain't that a hoot."

Jack pulled out Huck's watch, unconsciously running his finger over the cover's surface, and opened the case. It was two in the afternoon, and that beef jerky he had eaten in the saddle was getting thin. He closed the watch and dropped it back in his pocket. "You've been a big help. How much do I owe you for the horse? I don't expect being here more than a couple of days."

"Four bits for two days."

Jack fished a half dollar from his vest pocket and slapped it in the outstretched hand. "Thanks, Micah. I'll be back."

He untied his saddlebags and pulled his Winchester from the boot. He didn't figure on using the rifle, but he'd take it with him.

Jack raised his finger to the brim of his wrinkled and dirty Stetson. "See you later."

"Luck, Marshal."

Jack turned left out of the stables and headed down the boardwalk. He met several men, who nodded politely, trying not to stare. A lady, arms full of packages, almost dropped them when her eyes fell on his face. *I must be looking pretty bad,* he thought. Ahead, Jack saw a shingle announcing the Sheriff's Office. Reaching for it, he pulled the latch and stepped inside. A deputy, upon seeing Jack, almost choked on his coffee and started coughing. The sheriff, who had been examining wanted circulars, looked up.

His expression remained the same, taking in Jack's badge and then his cut and discolored face. He stood and extended his hand. "Marshal, don't mind my deputy. It ain't often he sees a man your size who's taken such a beating and wearing a U.S. Marshal's badge to boot. I'm Sheriff Tobias Rice."

Jack took the sheriff's hand. "Jack Sage, Sheriff." He gave the man a lopsided grin. "Sorry to upset him."

The sheriff waved Jack to a chair next to his desk and dropped back into his. "It's good for him. Nothing happens around here. He needs the excitement."

The deputy had regained his composure and nodded to Jack. "Afternoon, Marshal."

Jack nodded to him while keeping his eyes on the sheriff. "I'm after three men. They just rode into your town about four hours ahead of me, and I suspect they're currently enjoying the offerings of the Silver Dollar. I aim to corral them, and I'd like to use your jail."

The sheriff's chiseled face was clean shaven, though stubble had already darkened his sunbaked cheeks. Corners of his deep-set brown eyes sported distance wrinkles from squinting in the bright sun. His eyes didn't look away but were intent, searching. A thick neck was barely contained by his collar, and his shirt did little to hide the brute strength in the man's shoulders. Jack figured him to be about his age.

"You're welcome to use the jail." He nodded at Jack's face. "They the fellas who did this?"

Jack returned the nod. "The same. They also robbed the bank in Fort Smith and shot one U.S. Marshal and killed another. I aim to take them back for trial."

"That would be Judge Bell's court?"

"One and the same."

"Would you like some help?"

"I wouldn't turn it down. If I could get you and your deputy to cover whatever exits they may try to escape from, that would be a big help. They're also carrying quite a bit of money in three saddlebags. I'd like to make sure that money doesn't disappear in the confusion. You know, the magicians who work in saloons and brothels."

A hint of a grin crossed the lips of the sheriff. "That I do. You want to see a doctor first? I hate to say it, friend, but your face looks mighty uncomfortable."

This time, Jack grinned. "It's been better, but I'd like to corral these fellas before I take care of anything else."

"Good enough." The sheriff stood.

"One more thing. I want to emphasize the importance of taking these gents alive. They deserve to go back to Fort Smith and have a decent trial before they meet their maker."

"I couldn't agree more. Anything else?"

"Could I leave these things here?" Jack indicated his rifle and saddlebags.

"Sure, just lay your saddlebags on my desk, and I'll take your rifle."

Jack handed the man his Winchester. The sheriff stepped to his gun cabinet and set the rifle at one end. Before he could turn back, Jack spoke. "Could you hand me that Greener?"

The sheriff hesitated, then pulled the shotgun from the

cabinet and passed it to Jack. "I thought you weren't interested in gunplay? You use that thing, and a lot of innocent folks could get hurt."

"Intimidation, Sheriff." Jack broke the shotgun and extracted the two shells, tossing them back to the sheriff. "I'll be holding this in my left hand. I can draw faster than any of those three. If I have to shoot someone, it'll be with my handgun, not this shotgun, but you know how a man feels staring at these two black holes."

This time, the sheriff showed a wide grin. "I know I wouldn't want to be on the wrong end." He looked at his deputy. "Cyrus, you feel up to earning your money?"

"Yes, sir, Sheriff, I sure do."

Jack looked at the younger man. "Just remember. If one of them makes a dash, don't shoot him. I want all three of these men alive. Alright?"

The young deputy looked up at Jack. "Yes, sir, Marshal, alive." The deputy stepped ahead of the two other men and opened the door.

Jack motioned. "Lead the way, Sheriff. You know where we're going." The sheriff flipped the leather thong from his revolver and stepped through the door, Jack following.

The three men turned left and headed up the street, leaving the boardwalk clear for the citizens. The lawmen brought stares as their purposeful strides carried them toward the Silver Dollar.

"Marshal, the next building will be the Dollar. It has a regular front door. When you go in, there's a small foyer. The stairway is to the right of the room. The parlor, where your subjects are liable to be sitting, is also to the right and through an arched doorway. Get in there quick. Don't let any of the girls slow you down. The men may be upstairs, but they could also be in that parlor. There are two exits, one in back and one to the side. I'll be at the rear, and Cyrus will cover the side door."

Jack looked at the deputy. "Cyrus, I know I said I wanted them alive, but if your life is at stake, shoot to kill. They've already killed one U.S. Marshal and shot another. They won't hesitate to kill you, so don't give them the chance."

The deputy nodded. "Understood."

Sheriff Rice and Cyrus headed down an alley to get into position. Jack gave them a couple of minutes and stepped to the door.

He eared the hammers on the Greener back and shoved the door open. Two young women, scantily dressed, were waiting in the foyer. Their wide smiles disappeared when they saw the shotgun and Jack's face. With his right hand, he held a finger to his lips and motioned them out of the way. He scanned the stairway and landing at the top. No one was visible. Wasting no time, Jack stepped through the arched doorway to find Jed, the gang's leader, and his slow brother, Zeke, sitting on the brocade divan with three young women.

They were laughing and talking to the women. Each had a drink in his hand. They must have figured Jack was another customer, because neither turned toward him. He waited. It was at least a full minute before Zeke turned to the doorway and frowned.

17

Zeke gave a slow grin. "Howdy, Marshal. I told Jed not to kick you."

His brother spun around on the divan and froze. The shotgun's muzzles were less than six feet from his face. Jack returned Zeke's grin. "I sure wish he'd listened, Zeke, but I'm going to have to take you boys back to Fort Smith." Jack let his gaze drift to the women. "You ladies move over to that corner, out of the way of this Greener." He indicated the opposite corner from where he was standing.

They stood slowly, but once they were up, they dashed to the corner and stood there hugging each other.

Jack wiggled the shotgun. "Alright, boys, stand up." The two men wasted no time getting on their feet. *Amazing,* Jack thought, *the incentive a shotgun provides.* "You both know the drill. Drop your guns." Two gunbelts hit the floor with solid thuds. Jack moved back just far enough so he could see the bottom of the staircase. It was difficult, since the stairway was just on the other side of the parlor wall. Satisfied, he nodded at the girls. "One of you go to the side door and bring Cyrus in."

A blonde ran out of the parlor into what looked like the

kitchen and disappeared. A moment later, Cyrus walked in, his gun drawn. "Alright, Cyrus, keep an eye on these two." He turned to the girls. "Where's the other one?" They pointed upstairs. "Which room?"

A brunette spoke up. "He's in the third room on the left. Margaret is with him. Please don't hurt her."

Jack shook his head. "She'll be fine." Cyrus was on the kitchen side of the room, and the girls were in the corner formed by the kitchen wall. Jack was the only one who had a view of the stairway. He glanced back just in time to see a shadow cast from the wall lamp above the stairs. He went for his revolver.

Pain shot through his chest from the sudden movement. The ribs, though they were slowly mending, hadn't healed as well as they should because of the constant pounding of the horse's hooves. Jack cleared his holster and brought his revolver up as Vern, his weapon leading him around the corner, moved forward to bring his revolver to bear. He was too late. Jack fired. The roar of his revolver slamming off the plastered walls was deafening. The 216-grain solid-lead bullet from his .44 slammed into Vern's Colt, striking the cylinder broadside.

The blast of Jack's shot was overpowering in the small room, but the explosions of the five loads in Vern's .45-caliber Peacemaker sounded like a young war. The cylinder blew apart, blasting shrapnel throughout the house. The burning powder from the explosion set a curtain on fire, which could have burned the house to the ground except for the quick thinking of the brunette, who yanked the curtain down and threw a pitcher of water on it.

Fortunately, the shrapnel plowed into the walls and floors but found no flesh to harm other than Vern's. His hand disappeared in the blast, taking his wrist with it. The man dropped to the floor, screaming in pain and clutching at his forearm. His life as a right-handed fast gun was over.

Sheriff Rice dashed into the house, through the back door,

arriving at the base of the stairway along with Iris Hart, the owner and madam. Both stood aghast at the carnage throughout the two rooms. Blood and flesh were scattered everywhere, on the walls, hanging from the ceilings, and on the furniture. A finger hung sizzling on a hot lamp chimney.

Rice was shaking his head. "What the blue blazes happened?"

Cyrus pointed at the twisted piece of metal, all that remained of the Peacemaker. "Marshal Sage shot that feller in the hand, Sheriff. It set off all the loads in his weapon." He looked around the room in wonder. "Look what happened."

The two brothers had dove behind the divan when the weapon exploded. They were on their knees, only their eyes visible over the back.

Jack waved the Smith at them. "Get up and come around the couch."

The outlaws followed his direction, their eyes glued to their partner, who lay crying on the bloody floor. Bursting through the front door, the town marshal, followed by the doctor, dashed in. The marshal slid to a stop at the sight, and the doctor looked at the man on the floor and Jack. It appeared he had difficulty deciding who to take care of first. He decided on the gunman.

Jack nodded to the town marshal, "Howdy, Marshal," then turned to the two outlaws. "Alright, you two, where's the money?"

Zeke bent over.

"Easy, Zeke. You don't want to be reaching for a gun."

"Oh no, Marshal, I ain't reaching for no gun. I'm getting the money." He continued, taking a moment to gather them in one big hand, and raised the three saddlebags.

"Lay them on the couch."

Zeke did as he was told, his brother, Jed, staring longingly at the saddlebags.

Jack asked Jed, "Is that all of it?"

The bank robber pointed at Hart. "Except what I paid her. We ain't divided it up yet."

"How much did you pay her?"

Hart spoke up. "That money's mine. My girls worked for it, and look what you've done to my establishment. This is going to cost me a lot of money."

Jack's eyes stayed on Jed. "I asked you, how much did you pay her?"

"Two hundred dollars."

Jack shook his head. "Sheriff, that money belongs to hard-working folks back in Fort Smith. They would never elect to pay their money to Miss Hart or her establishment. Would you talk to her?" He turned to Cyrus. "Would you pick up the saddlebags and take this shotgun?"

"Sure, Marshal."

The younger man holstered his Colt, strode to the couch, picked up the saddlebags, and took the shotgun.

The exhaustion and injuries were catching up with Jack. He felt his strength waning, and thought, *I've got to hold on until I get these three in jail and the money in a bank.*

The beating, his injuries, and the long days in the saddle had sapped him of his strength. "Sheriff, could you take these fellas to jail and get that money to a bank? I'm running out of steam."

"Sure, Marshal Sage. I don't see how you've made it this far."

Jack moved to the divan and dropped to the seat. He gave a weak chuckle, "Me either," and leaned against the back. He had to make sure these outlaws got to jail and the money to the bank, but he remembered he had asked the sheriff to take care of everything. All he really needed to do was get to the hotel.

An unfamiliar voice made it into his consciousness. "Marshal Sage, I'm Dr. Ryan Porter. I'm going to take a look at your face. It might hurt a bit."

Jack felt light pushing and prodding at his forehead and cheek. *That shows what the doctor knows,* he thought. *It doesn't hurt at all.* He relaxed into the comfortable divan and surrendered to sleep.

Opening his eyes, his first thought was that they had gotten worse. Everything was red. The sheets, the spread, the curtains, and the walls, all red. He blinked and lifted his head. The bed squeaked, and a blonde woman, dressed in a red dress and sitting at the side of his bed, looked up from the newspaper she was reading.

Relieved, Jack saw she and her hair weren't red, and on further examination, the dresser and the door weren't either. He took a deep breath, his ribs giving him a sharp reminder of their damage. "Where am I?"

The young woman gave him a wide smile, exposing a gap where one of her front teeth used to be. "Why, Marshal, you're in the Red Room in the Silver Dollar. We had quite a time getting you up here." An eyebrow rose. "You are a big man. Dr. Porter ordered the sheriff to put you to bed here, but Mama Hart wouldn't hear of you sleeping in her bed without getting a good washing."

Jack lifted the bed covering. He was wearing a long nightshirt and nothing else. "Where's my clothes?"

"My, you are demanding, aren't you? The sheriff sent over your saddlebags. Mama Hart made us throw away those clothes you were wearing. She said they'd never get clean. We washed and ironed the ones you had in your saddlebags. They were all covered with trail dust." She rose, walked to the armoire, opened the door, and pointed to the hanging clothes. "See, all clean. Are you hungry?"

"How long have I been asleep?"

"Marshal, you slept throughout the day yesterday and all night." She leaned forward, examining his face. "I'd say the rest was good for your face. It's looking better."

Jack was not a prude. He'd never used the services of such a place as the Silver Dollar, but, in his line of work, he'd known quite a few women who, either by the need to eat, brutality, or greed, had found themselves working in a place like this. However, he had never spent a night in a brothel before, and he needed to be on his way. "What's your name?"

She smiled again, exposing the gap. "My name's Julie, Marshal. You feeling like a little company?"

Jack shook his head. "No, Julie, I am not. I'm feeling like I need to get about my business. If you'd step out of the room, I'll get dressed."

Opening the door, the girl gave him a pouting frown. "It ain't like I'd be seeing anything new."

When the door closed, Jack threw back the covers and swung out of bed. He changed quickly. Slipping them on, he felt the crispness of the clean clothes and appreciated the ladies' efforts. He felt even better when he picked up his hat. Someone had taken some time cleaning it. The dust and grime had been wiped off, and then it had been brushed, giving the Stetson a used but presentable appearance.

His badge hung over the edge of his right holster. Even it had been polished. Jack thought, *That's the best that badge has looked since I got it.* He slipped it on his clean vest and swung his gunbelt around his waist. After buckling the belt, he checked the loads. Both revolvers had been cleaned and reloaded. Feeling the best he'd felt since Jed had kicked him in the face, Jack opened the door and headed to the landing.

At the bottom of the stairs, he stopped. The room looked just as it had before Vern Lee lost his hand. The blood and gore were gone, and the walls were repainted, the burned drape was replaced, and the furniture was clear of any human remains.

Iris Hart, the madam, met him at the entrance to the parlor. "Well, lawman, you look a hundred percent better than you did yesterday. It's amazing what a little scrubbing and a good night's sleep can do for a man."

Jack felt his cheeks warm, and he didn't like it. His voice was gruff. "You took a liberty there, Miss Hart."

The woman, undeterred by his harsh tone, threw back her head and gave out a loud laugh. "Maybe more than you know, Marshal."

Jack could see she was needling him and appraising his reaction. He grinned. "Well, ma'am, whatever happened, it won't happen again. All I know is that after a good night's sleep, I feel better than I have in days."

"That's nice to hear, Marshal. Now all you need is a good meal inside that emaciated body."

"I'm thinking the same thing, ma'am. Where's a good place to eat?"

She pointed toward the kitchen. "We've got a nice big table in there and food the king of England wouldn't turn his nose up at. Now come on in and put the feed bag on."

Jack hesitated only for a moment, then thought, *What the heck. Food and a little information are what I'm after.* "Yes, ma'am, that sounds good, and may I say, you sure got this room straightened in a fine way and a short time. It looks mighty nice."

Iris beamed. "It does, doesn't it?" Grasping his arm and guiding him into the kitchen, she leaned toward him and spoke in a low, conspiratorial manner. "It pays to *know* the right people."

He couldn't help but grin at the statement. "I reckon you are right, ma'am."

She motioned to the chair at the head of the table. "Please sit there, Marshal. It's not often we have men who deserve to use that chair."

Jack knew when he was being handled, and he knew he was in the hands of a professional, in more ways than one. "Thank you. That's mighty nice of you."

He sat in the handmade wooden chair. It groaned a little, but held his weight. Immediately, a plate loaded with eggs, sausage, and potatoes was set before him by the brunette who had snuffed out the fire the day before. He looked up at her. "Thanks, that was quick thinking yesterday. If you hadn't got that curtain down and poured water on it, this place would have gone up like kindling."

At the compliment, she gave him a broad smile. "Thanks, Marshal. I just did what was needed."

Jack persisted. "You did more. In my business, I see all types of folks. Most have to think about something before they do it. You jumped right on it. If you were a man, I'd try to talk you into being a deputy for me. I'm not kidding."

Recognizing a sincere compliment when she heard it, the woman blushed. "Well, thank you again." To break the serious moment, she pointed at his plate. "Now eat those eggs before they get cold. Is five enough? I know a man your size has a big appetite."

Jack grinned, "That's a good start," and went to work on his breakfast.

She turned, opened the oven, and pulled out a steaming pan of biscuits. After dumping them into a basket, she set them in front of Jack. He watched them steam for a moment, then grabbed one, bouncing it in his hand before he went to work on the food.

Iris Hart sat next to Jack. She silently waited while he devoured the food.

Jack finished the fare on his plate plus four hot biscuits. Halfway through, the brunette placed a steaming cup of coffee on the table. Jack eyed the sugar bowl and pitcher of fresh cream, but the cup was full. He sipped it until he had drunk about a third of the coffee and went to work doctoring it.

Business must be slow this morning, Jack thought. Four more women had gathered in the kitchen, ostensibly to get themselves water, coffee, or something stronger.

"How about a piece of apple pie, if you have any room left?" Iris said.

Jack nodded to the women. "Morning, ladies," and continued,

"I always have room for apple pie, and I wanted to talk to you about that two hundred dollars."

Iris Hart's eyebrows went up in mock surprise. "Oh really, what about it would you like to discuss?"

The brunette set a huge piece of pie in front of him. "Thanks. That looks mighty good." He took a large bite, chewing it for a while before swallowing, then he turned to look directly at the madam. "Did you pay the sheriff that two hundred dollars?"

He could tell she was displeased with his question.

She answered, clipping her words short, "Yes, Marshal, I paid him."

Jack nodded. "That's good. The people of Fort Smith will appreciate your generosity."

Her frown deepened.

He took another bite of pie and chewed. When he swallowed, he washed the bite down with a sip of coffee and gave his head a single shake for emphasis. "That's mighty good coffee. I understand you have my saddlebags."

Voice more frosty than friendly, Iris said, "Yes, I do."

"Could you or one of your ladies bring them here, please?"

Iris said nothing, but looked at the blonde and gave a sharp motion with her head. Moments later the woman returned with the saddlebags. She tried to hand them to Iris, but again motioning with her head, the madam indicated Jack.

Jack took them. "Thanks." He moved the coffee cup and pie plate to the side and laid the bags on the table. After opening one side, he pulled out a heavy leather pouch. It clinked when he lifted it. "Ma'am, I appreciate you paying back that money. I'm not being sanctimonious when I say it belongs to those folks in Fort Smith, for it surely does. But this doesn't. It's mine."

Jack opened the pouch and began counting out bright gold double eagles. The madam's frown slowly switched to a smile as Jack stacked the gold. He made two stacks of five. Once he counted them out, he slid them across to Iris, who was now beaming. "That'll cover what the Anderson gang paid you."

Iris gazed at Jack. Sincere admiration and gratitude filled her eyes. "Marshal, I don't know how to thank you. I will not talk about expenses to you. I'm just going to say this really helps an old businesswoman."

Jack grinned at the madam calling herself a businesswoman. "I'm glad it helps." He reached into the pouch again, counted out five more, and looked at Iris. "Will a hundred dollars cover my use of your bed, the washing and cleaning, and the food?"

This time, Jack received a sincere smile from Iris. "Yes, Marshal Sage, it will more than cover the costs. You are quite generous. Thank you."

Jack closed the pouch and returned it to his saddlebags. There was a last piece of pie remaining on his plate. He forked it and stuffed it into his mouth, chasing it with his last sip of coffee. Standing, Jack looked around the room at the women. "Ladies, I'm sorry about shooting up your . . . uh . . . home, and I thank you for your hospitality. It's time to check on some prisoners. Have a nice day."

He had to run the gauntlet to get past the table, through the parlor, and out the door. Beginning with Iris, each one gave him a hug. Reaching the door at last, he pulled the latch and stepped outside. Two of Texarkana's female citizens were passing. Jack touched the brim of his hat and said, "Morning, ladies." In return, he received a "Humph" and two poisonous glares. Jack shrugged and headed to the sheriff's office.

18

Jack walked the short distance to the train depot and strode to the ticket window on the platform. Upon reaching the window, he had to lean down to see past the bars into the interior. Inside, a man wearing a green visor was working on papers at a counter. Jack called to him, "Could I get some information?"

The man, wearing a dark blue uniform with his green visor, stepped toward him. "How can I help you?" Seeing Jack's badge, the ticket agent added, "Marshal."

"I need to get to Fort Smith. I'll be transporting three prisoners and four horses."

The agent pulled out a schedule and studied it for several minutes, then began to write. He jotted down departure times and arrival times, including likely connections.

"Is there any problem hauling prisoners on your train?"

"None. It's done all the time."

"What about my horses?"

"Same with your horses. You'd be surprised at the number of folks who want their own horse when they arrive wherever they're going."

"Is there feed on board the train?"

"There'll be hay. Anything else you want, you'll have to provide it. We also take care of the water. As you can see, you'll be changing trains in Little Rock."

"Can I send a telegraph here?"

The man turned to the counter where he had been working, picked up a pad, and slid it across to Jack, then returned to his work at the counter. Jack first looked over the schedule the agent had given him. Surprised, he called the agent back. "Excuse me. If I catch the one o'clock train for Little Rock, I can be in Fort Smith at seven this evening?"

The agent wore spectacles, which balanced on the end of his pudgy nose. He reached under the bars for the schedule, looked it over, and slid it back to Jack. "Yes, sir. You will have a one-hour wait in Little Rock for the Fort Smith locomotive, but it will put you at your destination by seven."

"Thanks." Jack wrote out a message to Judge Bell and one to Grace. The agent had moved back to his counter work. Jack cleared his throat.

The man looked up, saw Jack was ready, and stepped back to the window. He took the two messages. After counting the number of letters in each message, he wrote a figure at the bottom of each sheet. Turning them around so Jack could see them, the agent looked up at Jack. "That'll be two dollars and eighty-five cents, Marshal."

Jack counted out the change and slid it across to the man. "When will they get the messages?"

"I'll send them as soon as you're finished."

"Can I pay for the tickets now?"

"Yes, sir, you sure can. In fact, you can bring your animals to the loading pen and keep them there until the train arrives, and we'll see they're loaded. I assume you'll be traveling in the coach with your prisoners?"

Jack nodded.

"Will you have anyone traveling with your animals?"

"Yep. I'll have him down here before loading time, so total is four tickets and four horses to Fort Smith, and one round-trip ticket."

The agent pulled out a thick book and from it made several notations. After totaling the figure, he slid a slip to Jack. "That'll be twenty-seven dollars and fifty cents."

Jack paid him, and the agent went back to his counter, operated a machine, and came back with a wad of tickets, keeping one separate. He held the single ticket and shook it. "This here is the round-trip ticket. The others are for the folks going to Fort Smith, and this is for the horses. Remember, they'll need to change cars, just like you will, in Little Rock. Be sure to be here in time for the one o'clock departure."

Jack took the tickets and stuffed them into his inside vest pocket. "Much obliged." He had a lot to do before one o'clock today, and he wanted to be on that train. He stepped out for the sheriff's office.

Sheriff Rice and Cyrus were sitting in the same chairs and doing the same thing when Jack had first seen them. They both looked up and grinned, with Rice speaking first. "Get a good rest?"

Jack returned the grins. "Slept right through. Woke up this morning, and they fed me. I couldn't believe how fast Iris got that place repaired and painted. No one would know. Yesterday, it was covered in blood and gore."

The sheriff shook his head. "She is a force to reckon with when she makes up her mind. People were jumpin' to get it finished for her. I'm not looking forward to the day I'll have to shut her down, but it ain't too far in the future."

"Well, she did right by me." He turned to Cyrus. "Did you get that money deposited?"

Cyrus swallowed his mouthful of coffee. "Yes, sir, I sure did. The sheriff has the receipt you'll need if you want to check on it.

That was a lot of money. It surprised me any bank in Arkansas, besides maybe Little Rock, would be holding that much."

Jack thought, *Yeah, a good portion of it was mine. I'm glad to have it back in the bank.* He nodded to the deputy. "I'm sure the Anderson gang thought they were set for life. All they had to do was kill a few people."

The sheriff responded, "Reckon their killing days are over. When are you taking them off my hands?"

"Pretty quick, Sheriff. I've got us all booked on the one o'clock through Little Rock to Fort Smith. You think you could have them down there in time to make the train? There's a lot to get done before it leaves."

Sheriff Rice leaned back in his chair and examined Jack's face. "You're looking better. You might stop in Doc Porter's office before you leave. He wanted to take a look at those stitches when you woke up, and yes, I'll have them at the train station in time."

"Obliged. I'll stop by if I have time. You can tell him I'll be seeing the doc in Fort Smith tomorrow. I've got another favor to ask."

Sheriff Rice raised his thick, black eyebrows.

"Can you spare Deputy Spencer to give me a hand to Fort Smith? He'll have to ride in the stock cars on the way up, but he'll have a ticket on the cushions for the return."

The sheriff looked at Cyrus. "Goodness knows I can spare him. All he does is drink coffee. Yesterday's the first excitement we've had for a long time. How do you feel about that, Cyrus?"

Cyrus had been listening, but his eyes were half-closed in the warm office. At the mention of a train ride, they popped open. "Sure, Sheriff. I'd be glad to help."

Jack pulled the wad of tickets from his vest and shuffled through them. Finding the loading pass and transfer for the horses and tickets for the deputy, he handed the paper to Cyrus. "Much obliged, boy. You'll make my job a lot easier."

Cyrus grinned at the tickets. "I ain't never rode a train before."

"It'll be an adventure. You can pick up the horses at the first stable coming into town from the north. The old gentleman's name is Micah. I've got a grulla named Smokey and the three horses those fellas rode into town." Jack tossed a thumb toward the jail door separating the sheriff's office and the cells. "You might get Micah to bring the tack down in a wagon. That'd make it easier. You'll have to transfer it in Little Rock. Might be easier there if you saddled all of them before the transfer. I'll have the prisoners, so I won't be able to help."

"Yes, sir, that ain't a problem at all. I'll take care of them."

Jack turned back to the sheriff. "Now I need to see the things you took off those fellas."

The sheriff pointed to his gun rack. "Besides yours, we took three Winchesters."

Jack stepped over and pulled his Winchester from the rack. "I'll be taking mine. You can have the others, plus their handguns, except for two Smith & Wessons."

"Yeah, I kinda figgered those two were yours." He pulled a desk drawer open, and after removing the two Smiths, he laid them on the desk, closing the drawer and looking up at Jack. "Am I right?"

Jack removed the saddlebags thrown over his shoulder, opened one side, and pulled two lightly oiled rags from the bag. Taking each Smith from his holster, he wiped it completely with one of the rags, then wrapped it in the same rag, and gently laid it in the saddlebags. Next, he stretched a long arm across the sheriff's desk and picked up each weapon. First, he broke each open to check the loads, then snapped it closed and dropped it into the proper holster. "Thanks, Sheriff. It feels good to have these two back."

"I can understand why. They shoot the .44 Henry cartridge. That's unusual."

"Yeah, a friend of mine who's a gunsmith in New Mexico

customized these. They're a fine pair. They fit my hands and load fast."

The sheriff picked up a sack at the side of his desk while he was nodding. "I understand. They get comfortable."

Jack laughed. "That's the word for it. I guess comfort gets more important as we get older."

The sheriff turned the sack on end, emptying its contents onto the desk. The first thing Jack spotted was his pocket watch. He picked it up, rubbing his thumb across the emerald exploding grenade.

"I'm sure glad to have this back. I was hoping they'd hang on to it, but you never know about their kind. They could've just as easily hung it in a tree and used it for target practice."

The sheriff held his hand out. "Could I see it?"

Jack had never had anyone ask him for his watch. There was a time he would have refused, but times had changed. "Sure." He handed it across to the sheriff, who took it and studied the emerald. "Is that a real emerald?"

"It is. My wife gave it to me when I was about twenty years old."

"It looks like a bomb blowing up."

"Close, it's an exploding grenade, the symbol of the French Foreign Legion." Jack had never talked much about his past, which also seemed to be changing.

Cyrus had risen and positioned himself where he could look over the sheriff's shoulder.

Surprised, the sheriff's eyes moved from the watch to Jack. "You were in the Foreign Legion?"

"Yep, mostly in Algiers and the outlying area."

Cyrus eyed the emerald and, in an awed voice, said, "The French Foreign Legion."

Jack smiled. "It's not romantic, Cyrus, it's hot and dusty, and you're living in a country where almost all the citizens hate you and want to kill you in the most horrific ways."

"But you said your wife gave this to you?" the sheriff asked.

"She did. It was only a short time after that she and my infant son were murdered, hacked to death with a sword. I found them in our home shortly after it happened."

Jack watched shock and horror fill the two men. The sheriff removed his hat. "Marshal, I didn't mean to bring back bad memories. I can't even imagine what it must be like living with such things."

Jack shook his head. "Don't concern yourself, Sheriff. That was a long time ago. It's much easier to talk about today than it was then."

"I can imagine."

Cyrus spoke up. "I'm sorry, Marshal, but I've got to ask. Did you find their murderers?"

Jack smiled. Not a friendly smile, but a smile of cold satisfaction. "Oh, yes, and back then, I was very good with a sword."

The room was silent as each man pictured the act of retribution, Jack knowing exactly what it looked and felt like, and even then realizing it wouldn't bring Yasmina and his son back.

"Well," Jack said, breaking the spell, "it's been good talking to you gents. Is there anything I need to know about the prisoners?"

The sheriff returned Jack's pocket watch and took a brown bottle that had been sitting on the bookcase next to the gun cabinet. "This is laudanum. Doc Porter left it for the younger fella. He dressed his hand and came by earlier this morning to check it again. He said the stump is doing fine, but the feller's in a lot of pain. If he starts hurting, to where he can't stand it, he's supposed to get a teaspoon full of this in a big glass of water. It won't knock him out, but he'll be plenty drowsy."

Jack nodded. "Anything else?"

The sheriff shook his head. "Not a thing. We'll see you at the station."

Jack slipped the bottle and spoon into his saddlebags and

touched his index finger to his hat brim. "Thanks for all your help."

The sheriff gave a barking laugh. "We didn't do much."

"Sheriff, you fellas were there when I passed out, and I understand you got me upstairs. I'm obliged. Now, can you tell me how to get to the bank?"

The sheriff gave him directions, and Jack stepped through the door into the morning sunshine. It was cool, but not cold, and the best thing, no rain was falling and the sky was clear. His wedding date was just around the corner. Hopefully, the Arkansas rain would stay away for a few more days.

~

JACK SAT behind the three men. The trip had been less enjoyable than he had expected, especially the portion from Texarkana to Little Rock, which seemed to go on forever. The engineer stopped every three or four miles, picking up folks or letting them off. He was surprised when they made their connection with time to spare. Though Cyrus had never ridden a train before, he was efficient in ensuring the horses were well looked after, and the train change with the animals was completed without a hitch.

The prisoners had been no problem. He had borrowed leg and wrist irons from the sheriff. Cyrus would return them. The three men seemed to be resigned to their fate, and created no ruckus, though Vern would occasionally begin moaning and asking for laudanum, which Jack gave him freely, just as the doctor instructed. Also, his sitting in the row behind the prisoners did away with the possibility of conversation, which made it a more relaxing trip other than the constant whistle blowing and the train stopping. Fortunately, there was much less of that type of delay from Little Rock to Fort Smith.

Jack did question Jed shortly after leaving Fort Smith. Leaning forward, where he could speak softly and not be heard by the other passengers, he asked, "Tell me, Anderson, how did you know Morgan? Was he a part of your gang?"

Jed Anderson shook his head. "No, sir. Morgan was just what he said he was, a station manager. We rode in there and made a deal to leave our horses before we hit the bank. We paid him ten bucks to keep 'em fed, watered, and ready. That was it. I figure he suspected something was going on, especially when we came barreling in to switch horses. We were mighty excited and talked about the bank robbery, even showed him the money, and he laughed right along with us. Then you and the other marshal came in. Marshal Sage, I've been thinking about this a lot, and I think you saved our lives. I think his plan was, as soon as we turned our backs, he was gonna blast us out of our saddles and take all the money. Yes, sir, I figger that was his plan."

Jack leaned back, thinking about Huck, killed by a civilian, who, at the sight of all that money, went bad. The train's whistle blew for the last time, pulling Jack from his thoughts.

They were approaching the Fort Smith station. Slowing, the platform gradually moved into view. Glancing ahead, he could see Buck, Nesbit, and a couple of other deputies, and there were Grace, Mary, and the boys. He was excited about seeing his family, but apprehensive about his appearance. He'd never minded how he looked. When he was a boy, he was big and gangly. Growing older, he knew he wasn't good looking. That was just the way God made him. But now, his face had been butchered up pretty badly. He had seen it in the mirror at the brothel. He grimaced inside, then chuckled and thought, *How am I going to explain spending the night at a brothel, and the ladies undressing me? I think that's something I should keep to myself.*

But, at the brothel, his glance in the mirror had given him his first look at what would be the new Jack Sage. It looked like the nurse, Sue Bryson, had done an excellent job of sewing the skin back to his forehead. While both sides appeared to be healing well, the left side seemed to be doing better than the right. The tear on the right angled in a jagged slash, running from his hairline down to the center of his right eyebrow. He didn't know if it was his imagination or the real thing, but it looked like a lightning bolt striking the ground in his eyebrow. *Oh, Grace,* he thought, *you are going to be so surprised. I hope you can take it.*

The train jerked to a stop, and Jack leaned forward. "You boys keep your seats until all the passengers are off the train."

The three nodded their heads, and the young fella who had his hand blown off spoke in almost a child's voice. "Marshal, this is starting to hurt real bad."

"You'll be settled pretty quick. Can you wait?"

The small voice responded, "I reckon."

The train emptied. Buck, leading Nesbit, came aboard. Buck was acting normal, so his head wound hadn't been a permanent injury other than the scar. The prisoners were sitting in front of Jack, and he waited to stand until the two deputies were close. When Jack stood, Buck's eyes locked on his forehead, and he stopped so fast Nesbit ran into him, cussing at him for stopping so quickly.

Buck ignored him. "Jack, goodness-gracious-sakes-alive, what the blue blazes happened to you?"

Jack poked Jed Anderson in the back of his neck with the muzzle of his Winchester. "He did. He put a boot and a spur in my face."

Buck's face darkened. Jed Anderson was sitting in the middle between Zeke and Vern. Buck reached across Zeke, who was on the aisle so he could stretch his long legs, grabbed the older brother by the front of his shirt, and dragged him into the aisle. He pulled the man's face within an inch of his. "You're the kinda man hangings were made for." He looked at Jack. "Is he the one who shot me?"

Jack shook his head. "Nope, that one was Cole Baker. He figured he could outdraw two Winchesters pointed at his gut."

"What about Huck's killer?"

"He's dead, too. Listen, Buck, I'm not going to give a full account on this train. Is there anyone helping that young deputy with the horses?"

Buck nodded. "Pauly and a deputy are back there."

"Good. I need to go thank him. Take these outlaws off my hands and let me go say hi to Grace and the boys first."

Buck shoved Jed back to Nesbit and jerked Zeke up. "Let's go."

Zeke turned his head so he could see Jack. "You take care of yourself, Marshal Sage. It was nice meeting you."

"You too, Zeke. I'll be seeing you."

Buck looked at Jack, his head tilted slightly to the right and his eyebrows lifted.

Jack just shook his head.

Lee rose, holding his stump, and Jack pulled the bottle of laudanum from his saddlebags, along with the spoon, and handed them to Buck. "This fella needs a teaspoonful of this stuff mixed with a full glass of water, and he needs it now. After that, every few hours or when he asks. He'll let you know when."

Buck took it. "What happened to him?"

"His Peacemaker blew up in his hand."

"Is that all you're gonna tell me?"

"That's all for now." Jack watched the prisoners slowly make their way to the forward exit. "I'll see you later and fill you in." He turned, going through the rear exit and down the steps. The family, that was the way he was thinking of them, was standing on the platform, aligned with the forward exit, and waiting.

Elijah saw him first and yelled, "It's Pa!" and dashed to him. He leaped into Jack's arms.

He caught the boy and gave him a big hug. "It's good to see you, son."

Elijah, excited and happy, yelled into his ear, "You too, Pa!"

Jack loved that word.

Billy came racing up right behind Elijah, and Jack grabbed him with his other arm. Though the boy was older and was growing out of hugs, he copied Elijah and threw his arms around Jack's neck. "Welcome home, Pa."

The boys filled Jack's heart with their greetings. He gave them a tight squeeze, then bent over to set them on the platform. When he raised his eyes, they met the emerald green eyes of Grace. His heart swelled even more. Not since Yasmina and his son had he felt such powerful emotions. Her eyes were opened wide and moist. He swept his hat from his head, removing the shadow over his damaged face.

19

Grace didn't break her stride. Reaching for Jack, she placed a hand on each side of his face, "My poor darling, welcome home," and pressed her lips to his. Warmth burst over Jack. The pain he still felt in his face disappeared, and all his being was wrapped in the kiss and embrace. He was over forty years old and had again found the love he had thought he would never have. The kiss continued until there was a loud "harrumph."

Jack could recognize that voice anywhere. The two broke their embrace, and Jack looked at the man standing ramrod straight behind Grace. "Judge, you seem to make it a habit of showing up at the wrong time." The judge was surrounded by the mayor and several town councilmen.

His entourage laughed uncomfortably, and Judge Bell even smiled. "Yes, well, that may be correct, but I wanted to congratulate you for bringing these bank robbers and killers to swift justice. You did well, Jack, and your good mayor would like the opportunity to express the gratitude of your friends and neighbors for recovering their hard-earned money."

Jack thought, *Mine too, and my gosh, if the mayor is more long-*

winded than the judge, how long are we going to be stuck out here? Look at this crowd. It keeps growing. Heaven keep me from politicians.

The mayor stepped forward, looking around at the growing crowd. "Marshal Sage, it is with pleasure that I give you, from the hearts and souls of the fine people of Fort Smith, Arkansas, and to demonstrate our sincere gratitude for your unrelenting efforts through your own pain and suffering, this key to our fair city." The mayor had been standing with his hands behind his back. When he mentioned the key, he brought a monstrous gold-painted wooden key around and held it up for everyone on the platform to see.

A cheer burst forth from the crowd.

The thought ran through Jack's mind, *That actually sounds sincere. I guess I'd be cheering if someone brought back my life savings.*

The mayor leaned forward. "You might wave to the crowd."

Jack hadn't thought of waving, but it made sense to acknowledge their thanks. He raised his right hand and waved it back and forth to the people.

The mayor ceremoniously bowed and held the key out to Jack.

Grace whispered, "Take the key, Jack."

He took the key from the mayor and waved it eliciting another loud cheer. After one more wave, he allowed it to drop to his side, Elijah and Billy taking it and examining it with youthful curiosity.

The mayor, who had never met him and had a hard time keeping his eyes off Jack's facial injuries, took his right hand and shook it vigorously. "Thank you, Jack. You saved a number of our citizens' life savings by bringing this money back to our town."

Jack's reply was simple. "That's what I do, Mayor."

"Yes, but thank you." He turned to the crowd. "That's all, folks. Let's allow the marshal to get home and relax. I'm sure he's tired after what he's been through."

The crowd began to dissipate, and the judge stepped close to

Jack. "Would you be able to stop by tomorrow, say, about ten in the morning?"

Jack was surprised the judge was being so gracious, and it wasn't a late night order to see him in his office. "Sure, I'll be there at ten."

Judge Bell tipped his hat to Mary and Grace, turned, and was gone.

Grace, whose arm had been around Jack's waist since the spectacle had begun, swung back and planted another kiss on him, which elicited a sharp comment from Billy. "Ma, you're in public."

"Yes, she is," Mary said, stepping forward.

Grace stepped back, and Mary gave her future son-in-law a hug and kiss on the cheek. "Welcome back, you poor man. It looks like you got the short end of the stick."

The boys were on each side, hanging onto his gunbelt.

"It feels like it, too. I hope I'm not too ugly for you folks."

"Don't be ridiculous, Jack. You might have some scars, but they just make men look stronger. Now let's all go home."

"Just a minute." Jack looked around. Cyrus was standing off to the side, away from all the hoopla. Jack motioned him over, glancing at Grace and then Mary. "Do you have room for another guest tonight? I know it's late, but do you think you could feed him?"

Grace and Mary saw the young deputy walking toward them. Mary nodded, and Grace said, "Of course we do, and we'd be glad to." She smiled. "We're going to be feeding you."

Jack pulled Cyrus into the group. "What about the horses?"

"Yes, sir. A man by the name of Pauly and one of them deputy marshals took them off my hands. They all traveled well, and I think your horse was especially happy to see that Pauly feller."

"Good. I appreciate you taking care of them." Jack directed the deputy's attention to the women. "Cyrus, this lady is Mary

Nelson, and this is her daughter, Grace Blakely." He nodded at the two boys at his side. "These are my sons, Billy and Eli."

Eli thrust out his hand, and Billy followed his example. "Howdy," the boys said in unison.

Cyrus took each hand, giving each one a shake. "Howdy, Eli. Howdy Billy."

After Cyrus straightened, Jack continued. "Folks, this young fella helped me corral the outlaws and bring them back. He is Deputy Cyrus Spencer from Texarkana. Cyrus, these two ladies own the absolute best boardinghouse you'll find anywhere around. Even better, they have a vacancy tonight, and they are known for their good food." Before the deputy could say anything about money, Jack continued, "My expense account will cover your stay, so don't worry about funds. How does that sound to you?"

Cyrus had shucked his hat from his head when he was introduced. "Marshal, I don't reckon I could come up with a better deal if I tried. It's nice to meet you ladies, and thank you."

Grace gave him a dazzling smile. "You are more than welcome, Cyrus. We are going to Ma's Bed and Eats right now if you would care to join us."

He glanced at Jack, who gave a nod. "That'd be real nice, ma'am."

Mary led the way. Cyrus, Eli, and Billy followed with Grace and Jack bringing up the rear.

Eli looked up at his new acquaintance. "You're from Texarkana?"

Cyrus shot him a grin. "I sure am, lived there my whole life."

Billy put in, "Is it really divided by the state line, half Texas and half Arkansas?"

"It is, and that can sure cause confusion sometimes."

"How's that?"

Cyrus had the boys breaking out in laughter with his tales. ". .

.up that blamed tree with Mrs. Wilson's tabby showing me a fine set of teeth."

Grace had taken one of Jack's arms in hers. She smiled up at the big man and mouthed, "Welcome home."

~

JACK SAT in Judge Bell's office, listening to the judge go on about the importance of his having caught the bank robbers, and how it would be a terrible thing for him to leave Fort Smith permanently. He pulled out his pocket watch, glanced at the emerald, and opened it to check the time: ten thirty.

The judge stopped, eyeing Jack's watch. "Am I boring you, Marshal Sage?"

Jack closed the watch and dropped it back into his vest pocket. "No, Judge, of course not. It's just that I have a lot to do and not much time to do it in. Mary has the wedding scheduled in church for the first of May. You understand, Judge, that's just three days away."

"Jack, I want to get this trial finished and out of the way. I can schedule it for tomorrow. You can testify, and if they're sentenced to death, they can be hanged the next day."

"Great, that's just great. You want to hang a man who doesn't even really understand why he's being hanged, and a young fella whose hand I shot off, and you want to do it the day before my wedding. What a great way for Grace and me to remember our vows."

Bell had been pacing. He stopped and glared at Jack. "What the blazes has gotten into you? A hanging is a hanging. It doesn't affect anything else."

It was Jack's turn to stare, this time in disbelief. "Judge, have you become that callous? Of course it affects everything. Don't you notice the good people of this town, how subdued they are, how they go about their business in a somber mood for days after a hanging? You can't say a hanging doesn't dampen folks' spirits. That's crazy." Jack jumped up and started for the door.

"Wait, Jack, wait, please."

Jack stopped. He turned to the judge, eyebrows raised. "Yes?"

"How long will you be gone to Little Rock?"

"We leave on the late train on the first and return on the eighth."

The judge stopped pacing and returned to his big leather chair behind his desk. After lowering himself into his padded chair, he began consulting his calendar. "The eighth. When are you pulling out for Texas?"

"Monday, May fifteenth, and when are you planning on making Buck marshal?"

The judge looked up. "Don't you think that's my business?"

Jack shook his head. "Just tell me the date, Judge. In fact, you should have included him in this meeting." Jack pointed at the couch. "He should be sitting right there, and you know it. What's the holdup?"

The judge leaned back. "I have a bad feeling about Buck. He's been shot in the head. It might make him crazy at any time."

Jack returned to and sat in a wingback chair in front of the judge's desk. "Judge, that's what's crazy. I've—"

Bell pointed an index finger at Jack when he spoke. "That's twice you've called me crazy. Don't do it again."

Jack took a deep breath while thinking, *I've got to calm down. Just a few more days. What I'd love to do is reach across this table and bend that finger so far back it's pointing at him. Calm down.* He took another breath. "Alright, Judge. You're right. It won't happen again, but your expectation about Buck is unreasonable." Jack yanked his hat off and turned so the judge could get a close look at the back of his head. He laid his palm into an indentation in his skull. "You see that?"

Bell had leaned forward. His eyes opened wide with concern. "My goodness, Jack, what happened?"

"A man I trusted slammed me in the back of my head with the butt of a Spencer. I'm lucky it didn't kill me. A rancher found me, and his family nursed me back to health. That's been several years ago, and I'm not crazy yet. He isn't going crazy! You've got to trust that man. He's the best man you've got."

"Except you."

Jack rolled his eyes, straightened, slapped his hat back on his head for emphasis, and leaned back in the chair. "I'm done, so forget about me. Buck knows his business. The only problem I had with him was his aggressiveness, but being ambushed has made him more cautious. Not too much. Just the amount he needs. That's called experience, exactly what I've heard you say you wish he had. And in a weird way, it has brought him more respect from his men. The older men are ready to accept him. He's always been good, but now he's better."

"What about the paperwork?"

"He's better than me."

The judge blew out a sharp blast of air, slammed his pen down, and glared at Jack. "Alright." He looked at the door and shouted, "Nesbit!"

Within moments, the deputy was pushing the door open. "Right here, Judge. By the way, I reckon they can hear you two in Little Rock."

The judge frowned and lowered his voice. "Would you get Buck for me?"

"Yes, sir. I think I saw him downstairs just a few minutes ago."

Deputy Nesbit was gone only a couple of minutes when they heard steps coming up the stairway. The door opened, and Buck walked in, pushing the door closed.

Judge Bell didn't waste any time. "Buck, are you ready to be the United States Marshal over this territory?"

Buck looked at Jack.

Jack shot him a frown. "Don't look at me. He's the one asking you."

Buck turned back to the judge. "Yes, sir."

"Then raise your right hand."

Judge Bell gave Buck the oath from memory, and Buck answered, "I do." The judge opened his desk drawer and pulled out a badge. He tossed it to Buck, who removed his deputy badge, started to put it in his pocket, but saw Judge Bell with his hand out. He stepped forward, placed the badge in the judge's hand, and pinned the marshal's badge to his vest.

Jack was standing within reach of Buck, but waited for the judge to come around his desk.

"Let me be the first to congratulate you, Buck. You deserve this."

"Thank you, Your Honor."

Jack extended his hand. "Congratulations, Buck."

He grinned at Jack. "I heard you yellin'. You just want out of the paperwork."

Jack laughed. "You caught me." He turned to Judge Bell. "Are you through with me, Judge?"

The judge looked surprised, but only for a moment. He extended his hand, and Jack took it. "Jack, I want you to know I appreciate all you've done, but I am so glad to be finished with all of your arguing."

Jack grinned as he shook the judge's hand. "Me too, Your Honor." He opened the door, stopped, and looked back. "Seriously, Judge, don't hang those boys before my wedding. In fact, if they hang, the best time would be while we're in Little Rock. If you could work that out, I'd be much obliged."

"Wait," the judge replied. "What if we had the trials tomorrow so you could testify, and if any hangings result from them, we can execute them on the sixth? That will give you a day of grace, in case something happens to the train schedule."

Jack felt relief flood over him. As much as Jed needed to hang, he didn't want it to happen around the wedding. Grace's wedding day would be marred for life. "Your Honor, I can't tell you how much I appreciate that. Thanks."

Judge Bell's tense face relaxed into a smile. "Good. You know I'm doing this for Grace."

Jack grinned. "I do. I owe you."

Jack watched Bell's eyebrows shoot up and instantly replied, "But not enough to stay. What time do you want me in the courtroom tomorrow?"

The judge rubbed his chin, thinking about the question. Finally, he responded, "Why don't you show up here around nine o'clock? If I need you sooner, I'll send Nesbit."

"Sounds good." Jack locked eyes with Judge Bell. "I'm serious, Judge. I won't stay, but I owe you personally." He stepped out of the office and pulled the door closed. Nesbit wasn't at his desk. Jack shrugged and started down the stairs. Feeling like a huge weight had been lifted from his shoulders, Jack smiled to himself and thought, *Not only will Grace not have the memory of a hanging, but I'm out of the law business, I'm getting married in three days, and we'll be heading for Texas in no time.* Jack was so happy his big, six-foot-four-inch frame was skipping down the stairs like Elijah or Billy. He reached for the door, and the crash of a large-caliber handgun erupted just outside.

His revolver leaped into his right hand, and he charged out the door. On the boardwalk, next to the alleyway, lay Nesbit, blood pouring from a bullet wound in his neck. Jack made it to the man in four running strides. From the angle of the deputy's head, Jack could tell the man's spine was destroyed. His unseeing eyes stared into the sunlit sky.

Jack felt a combination of despair at the loss of a friend and an all-encompassing rage. He tore past his friend in time to spot a face before it disappeared around the end of the building. He barreled down the alley, feeling the blood rising much as a jungle cat before it leaps on its fleeing prey.

At the last second, his experience took over, and instead of racing around the corner, he dove, low and fast, his momentum carrying him into a slide in the rainless, dry, pulverized dirt. In mid-leap, when asked later why he did it, all he could say was instinct. He also drew his left Smith & Wesson, pulling back the hammer.

Shock flashed through his mind when he saw the big man standing in front of him, only ten feet away. The thought the killer might be this man had only momentarily passed through his mind, because he knew the killer would want to face him in public, hoping to humiliate him and kill him in front of an audience. *But he fooled me,* Jack thought.

The man fired his first shot when Jack appeared from around the corner, but he fired high. The bullet flew several feet above Jack, who slid through the dirt, his left Smith & Wesson centering on the killer's chest. Jack could see him correcting, dropping the muzzle of his Colt to Jack's level. The man's lips were drawn back, exposing his teeth in a grimace of hate and what had been excited pleasure. Now, with the bullet's miss, the excitement had turned to surprise and fear.

Jack's left revolver was unhampered from the pull of the ground caused by his powerful slide, which affected his right arm and weapon. Before the muzzle of the man's Colt could cover Jack, the lawman pulled the trigger. Fire belched from the weapon even as he slid to a stop, stabilizing his right hand and firing with the right-hand weapon. Both bullets drove into the killer's body. He was pushed back, but remained on his feet. Jack continued firing, left and right together, watching the man try to bring his weapon to bear even as he was being pummeled by bullet after bullet. "You'll never kill another man!" Jack shouted and continued to fire again and again until both of his smoking weapons started clicking, hammers falling on dead chambers.

A hand grasped his left forearm. "Jack, he's dead. You can stop shooting. He won't kill again."

Jack rotated his big head to see Buck standing at his side,

concern filling his eyes. He nodded, dropped one weapon into its holster, broke the other open, and began pulling cartridges from his belt until the Smith was fully loaded. He changed weapons, repeated the procedure, and dropped the second revolver home in its holster. People had begun gathering around. Gasping at the bloody corpse lying on the ground in back of the courthouse, but the gasps weren't at the blood and gore. They were at the recognition of the killer who had murdered so many deputy marshals.

20

Barrett Clagg, the ex-prominent business owner turned killer, lay dead in the dirt. The man whose brothers had harassed, robbed, and killed greenhorns headed west, even Elijah's family. The man who, in a gunfight, Jack had refused to kill and instead, like Vern, had allowed him to live, giving Clagg a chance to change his life.

It didn't work, Jack thought. *Maybe, after the death of his brothers, he just had too much hate to change.* He turned to Buck. "Nesbit's dead."

Buck, staring at the riddled body of Clagg, nodded. "I know. This piece of trash killed him and so many other good lawmen." He looked up at Jack. "I thought you said it wouldn't be Clagg, that he wanted to humiliate you."

Jack shook his head, still staring at the dead body of the evil man. "I was wrong. He was so filled with hate. He must've wanted all lawmen dead. I think he would have continued if he hadn't caught sight of me entering the alley. It was a snap decision. His hatred of me overcame his bloodlust to kill lawmen."

Jack, his voice hard and bitter, spoke to the body. "Big mistake,

Clagg. As bad as you thought you were, I've had more experience at killing, at ambushes. Big mistake."

The judge had walked up in time to hear Jack talking to the dead man. He looked at Buck, who gave a brief shake of his head. The judge said nothing. Buck turned to the big lawman. "You alright, Jack?"

Jack's head turned slowly, and he focused on Buck. His steel-gray eyes warmed, and a sardonic grin barely lifted the corner of his mouth. "Yeah, Buck. I am now."

He lifted his eyes above Marshal Buck Walker to see Grace running down the alley. His mind went to the wedding. He brushed Buck aside and started toward her, taking a deep breath. She was lovely. Relief covered her face. Her full red lips spread into a wide smile, deep black curls bounced with every running step, and her bright green eyes promised a lifetime of love.

The crowd separated, allowing her to reach him. He swept her into his arms and pulled her so close he could feel her heartbeat. *I'll feel that heartbeat as long as I live,* he thought. Jack loved her scent, the smell of bread and roses.

She pulled his head close to her lips and whispered, "I love you, Jack Sage. Would you please stop scaring me?"

He felt his stubble grate across her soft cheek. His lips touched her ear. "I love you, too. I'm done with killing," but in that instant an unbidden thought arose, *At least for now*. His thick arms squeezed her tighter, and the big lawman pushed the thought from his mind.

Jack Sage finally has an opportunity to live his life with love and family–or does he? Ride with Jack in his new adventure.

Book 8:

Honor of the Star

If you loved the Logan Mountain Man series and have lamented the series ending at three books, I have good news for you. The series has been resumed and the next book in the Logan Mountain Man series can be ordered today.

Book 4

Burden of a Mountain Man

AUTHOR'S NOTE

I hope you've enjoyed reading *Justice of the Star,* the seventh book in the Jack Sage Western Series.

If you have any comments, what you like or what you don't, please let me know. You can email me at: Don@DonaldLRobertson.com, or fill in the contact form on my website.

www.DonaldLRobertson.com

I'm looking forward to hearing from you.

Reviews on Amazon are also appreciated.

I look forward to sharing Book 8 of the Jack Sage Western Series, Honor of the Star, with you in the near future.

Also, if you enjoyed the Logan Mountain Man series, get ready for the new adventures of Floyd Logan. He will soon be loose in the Rocky Mountains again.

Have a terrific day.

BOOKS

A Jack Sage Western Series

STRANGER WITH A STAR

WITHOUT THE STAR

RETURN OF THE STAR

THE HANGING STAR

FIVE WOMEN AND THE STAR

THE LOYAL STAR

JUSTICE OF THE STAR

HONOR OF THE STAR

Logan Mountain Man Series

(Prequel to Logan Family Series)

SOUL OF A MOUNTAIN MAN

TRIALS OF A MOUNTAIN MAN

METTLE OF A MOUNTAIN MAN

BURDEN OF A MOUNTAIN MAN

Logan Family Series

LOGAN'S WORD

THE SAVAGE VALLEY

CALLUM'S MISSION

FORGOTTEN SEASON

TROUBLED SEASON

TORTURED SEASON

Clay Barlow - Texas Ranger Justice Series

FORTY-FOUR CALIBER JUSTICE

LAW AND JUSTICE

LONESOME JUSTICE

NOVELLAS AND SHORT STORIES

RUSTLERS IN THE SAGE
BECAUSE OF A DOG
THE OLD RANGER

Printed in Dunstable, United Kingdom

83126998R00122